W. H. (William Henry) Shelton, Richard H. (Richard Hooker) Wilmer

A Man Without A Memory

W. H. (William Henry) Shelton, Richard H. (Richard Hooker) Wilmer

A Man Without A Memory

ISBN/EAN: 9783741118067

Manufactured in Europe, USA, Canada, Australia, Japa

Cover: Foto ©Andreas Hilbeck / pixelio.de

Manufactured and distributed by brebook publishing software
(www.brebook.com)

W. H. (William Henry) Shelton, Richard H. (Richard Hooker) Wilmer

A Man Without A Memory

A Man Without a Memory

And Other Stories

A Man Without a Memory

And Other Stories

BY

WILLIAM HENRY SHELTON

NEW YORK

CHARLES SCRIBNER'S SONS

1895

`

TROW DIRECTORY
PRINTING AND BOOKBINDING COMPANY
NEW YORK

To

My Dear Friend

Mrs. Louis Livingston Seaman

who more than any other is
interested in its publication, this book
is lovingly dedicated

January 21, 1895

CONTENTS

A Man without a Memory

A MAN WITHOUT A MEMORY

I

I WAS so completely at a loss about the points of the compass that while the sun was, perhaps, three hours above the horizon on my right hand, I had no means of judging whether the time were nine o'clock in the morning or four o'clock in the afternoon. I was seated alone in a rickety old buggy, driving, or at least holding the reins over a horse evidently weak with age, whose only possible gait was a walk, except when at the foot of a hill his weakness yielded for a space to the pressure of the wagon and he fell into a listless trot, which presently subsided into the original walk. Where I had come from, or whither I was going, or where or how I had come into possession of the nondescript equipage, were alike unknown to me. The heat of the sun warmed me comfortably. The fields had an agreeable smell, and the oppressive stillness in which one of the wheels of the wagon creaked mournfully, and the hoofs of the old horse paddled the dusty road with shuffling beats, filled me with a vague surprise, as if I had just awakened from a dream of turmoil, and had but half awakened at that, because I seemed to dimly realize that I was not yet in the full possession of my normal faculties.

I was scarcely more ambitious than the horse which was drawing me. A vague idea that mine was a case of suspended animation began to take hold on my mind. How else could I account for my possession of the horse and wagon, and for my mysterious surroundings? The only moving object in sight was a carriage behind me, which I could see contained two men, whose horse was making no better time than my own. The approach of the two men had no interest for me. I was struggling too hard to grasp myself. It was my recollections of the events which seemed to be last past, now growing rapidly more distinct, that were helping me to re-establish my identity. My eye fell on my left shoe, from which the sole was torn away at the toe, and straightway I remembered that the morning before I had struck it on a sharp stone imbedded in the road; but then I had been marching with my companions with a gun on my shoulder, we

had just passed at a swinging step through the
long street of a village. I remembered the
houses of stone and hewn logs standing close
on the road, with closed doors and blinds, the
cheering of the men belonging to other divis-
ions who were lounging on the rough flagging
behind their stacked muskets as we swung by,
the crowds of officers and the ranks of held
horses which choked the public square in front
of the brick building where army head-quarters had been established.

Then I remembered how, without a moment's
rest or refreshment, we had been pushed to the
front, to re-establish a yielding line. I could
feel again the cold chill that ran through my
hair as the first rifle balls whistled with a hot,
spiteful sound past my ears, and then the excitement and exaltation when time flew with such
unaccountable rapidity that a day, in passing,
shrank to the dimensions of an hour ; while in
recollection it was fraught with incidents sufficient to crowd a week, when, however you may
account for it, early morning stumbled over
midday without any perceptible interval between, and you suddenly found yourself fam-
ished and fell to eating with one hand in your
haversack, and the other on your rifle. I remembered that on this morning, which should

have been yesterday, I had been doing all these things—fighting, running, shouting, building up small granite ledges into breast-works, dimly conscious of the dead and wounded on every hand. The roar of artillery and musketry had been deafening, and the pungent sulphurous smoke rolled in white clouds along the crests of the fields, and rose like steam from the standing corn, hot and stifling to breathe. How vividly the awful scenes surged up in my mind ! Where had I slept since ? I remembered that we had rallied and charged across the open ; what an intense relief I felt when the regiments had leaped down into a sunken road, and we took refuge behind the opposite bank. I could see the appealing eyes of the wounded boy lying close to the edge of the smoking grass, at whose body the rushing line had parted and closed again. I was panting, grimy and perspiring, against the gravelly bank. A thorn - tree spread its branches above my head, and the earth beneath me was strewn with green boughs, as if a tempest had been raging there. Through the rails of the low fence, I saw a shattered gun limber with one mangled horse leaning against the pole, his mates and masters heaped on the ground about him—the whole group cut sharply against the sky.

I remembered how crowded we were in that narrow lane, and how grateful we felt for the rest and protection it afforded us in our exhaustion, as if we had been a great suffering body suddenly relieved of intense pain ; then how the drowsy sense of security was rudely dashed by the awful scream of a shell which came swelling from the front—hissing, rushing, roaring until, as it passed above the fences over our heads, it sounded like the flight of a steam-engine through the air. The cannoneers who were sending us these spiteful compliments from the crest of a distant hill, were beyond the reach of our rifles. If we looked over the bank we could see, at intervals, a puff of white smoke against the rim of the woods, and a hot flash of fire bursting through the small white cloud, followed by a dull report, and then the screaming crescendo of the oncoming shell which culminated above our heads, and then died away behind us. Once a shell burst in front of our position, a cloud of dust floated over us, and a shower of leaves and branches fluttered down from the thorn-tree over my head.

I remembered how we laughed and made light of this grim annoyance, and felt a renewed security in our natural earthwork, and counted with glee the splintered places on the board

fence behind us. I remembered the first inti-
mation of the attack of the infantry, coming in
the form of a thin skirmish fire puffing from the
crest in front—the balls pattering on the fences
—then the dark line rising above the ridge,
with flags and glittering bayonets — and then
the onrush and the wild cheering — and then
how we reserved our fire until they were close
upon us—and how the line withered and broke
under that smoking volley, leaving the wounded
scattered on the hill, and how they came again
and again only to be rolled back, covering the
hill thicker and thicker with the dead—how
we cheered and yelled and leaped on the fences
at each bloody repulse—and how some of the
wounded almost crawled to the shelter of our
fence.

I remembered how steadily they formed for
the last charge just beyond the smoking weeds,
in full view and in close range from our secure
position, and how we laughed and jeered and
admired them, and held our fire to give them a
fiercer welcome than ever when they should
come. Everything I saw and everything I
thought in those critical moments seemed to be
burned into my memory. The familiar device
of the old flag with the red stripes and blue
field of stars, on which that broken line was

dressing, carried me back to the days when I had cheered it and sang to it, as enthusiastically as I now jeered it and cursed its upholders through the powder-blackened rails of the fence, and across the belt of smoke and fire which smouldered in the dry turf of the bank.

Just as they started with a cheer, a gust of hot air swept the smoke in our faces, and impelled little tongues of flame to leap up and consume solitary dry weeds, and simultaneously we heard a blast of bugles from the right, and saw an awful vision of whirling horses galloping and turning in a cloud of dust at the end of that sunken road. The sunlight flashed on brazen guns and polished tire, and the bobbing heads of the drivers, as they lashed their teams to the rear, passed and repassed each other like figures in a fiendish dance. I remembered that instant of horror which impelled some to spring on the banks and fences, regardless of the charging infantry, and completely paralyzed the faculties of others — the mingled cries of warning and reproach—a glaring burst of flame —a deafening roar, a benumbing concussion which for an instant made my head fill all space, and along with it a sickening sensation of drowning in the air, and then darkness.

In the next instant, as it seemed to me, my

eyes opened dimly on a great field hospital. It
was chill night, and men with lanterns were
moving to and fro along the lines of wounded,
and in and out of the lighted farm buildings.
Ambulances were unloading, fires were burning,
men were moaning, laughing, cursing, cooking
—I smelt the fragrant odor of coffee and frying
meat. I saw men with pale begrimed faces sitting up in the glare, exchanging canteens and
wetting bandages. I heard moaning and talking behind my head and the shifting of restless
bodies on the straw. Just before me I saw the
active figures of surgeons working over lighted
tables. I was dimly conscious of all this, but
without the power to speak or move. I could
only see those objects which came within the
radius of my limited vision, and the firelight
shining up into the branches of the tall trees,
and the quivering stars in the dark heavens beyond, were more directly before my eyes. The
men stretched close about me were utterly silent. I heard the wind soughing in the tree-
tops and the tinkling of water in the spring-
house sounding through groans and imprecations,
and for once I seemed to hear with my parched
tongue instead of with my ears. Outside the
tantalizing tinkling of that water going to
waste, I seemed scarcely interested in what was

going on about me, and even to that I became more and more indifferent. A delightful lethargy soothed my limbs and faculties. I was like one conscious of falling asleep.

The attendants from the tables brought another body and laid it down beside me. I knew that I lay in a row of such ; I was indifferent. The men retired whence they came, the busy surgeons vanished, the firelight died out in the tree-tops, the twinkling stars paled in the heavens beyond, the tinkling water sounded farther and farther away, as if the spring-house had been retreating up the hill—and darkness enveloped me again.

I had shut my eyes to recall this vision, and presently they reopened on the jogging horse and the sunlit road, and I experienced the sensation of relief that comes to one awaking from a frightful dream. The dry hub was creaking as before, and the jingling bolts and rattling thills had a delightfully reassuring, even a musical sound. I alighted and walked around my turnout. It was dilapidated surely, and muddy as country vehicles are apt to be. I had not thought of my gun before, but to my inexpressible relief the barrel of a musket protruded from the boot, lying softly across a coil of blanket. I recognized neither of these prop-

erties as my own; even my belt and cartridge-
box had a strange look, but these equipments
might have been changed in hospital or supplied
to me after my recovery. I certainly had recovered. The recollection of the fragment of
shell which had struck my head in the sunken
road came vividly to mind, and I instinctively
plucked off my hat and passed my other hand
softly over that part of my scalp where I thought
the wound should be. I rather expected to feel
a mass of clotted hair, but instead my fingers
brushed over a surface as smooth and polished
as ivory; but there was indeed a tender place.
The surgeons had shaved my head in the process of recovery. I must have been insensible
for a considerable time.

The old gray horse was stamping his feet
and shaking his headstall at a green fly which
was buzzing about his withers, and he had
whisked the reins into the road while I had
been examining the wagon. The harness had
high, rusty hames and a saddle surmounted
with square, tarnished german - silver turrets,
and was altogether as antiquated as the wagon.
It was all beyond my understanding, and the
two men following me in the carriage had been
halted all this time, in the most exasperating
way.

I had but one desire, which was prompted
by my sense of duty in the matter of returning
promptly to my regiment. In that respect my
conscience would be satisfied, if only I used
my best endeavor to return ; so I gathered up
the reins and took my seat in the wagon, and
the old horse cheerfully resumed his walk.
My late experience with my command had
been so terrible, that I was forced to admit
to myself the relief I felt in my present peaceful surroundings and comfortable style of
marching.

The sun on my right hand was lower than
when I had first noticed it. It was certainly
declining. That, then, was the west, and I
was driving into the south. I preferred to
drive south. I felt some surprise at the warmth
of the evening, but everything was disjointed
and surprising. In front of me was a broad
wheat-field where the yellow bundles lay thick
in the stubble between the strips of green
oats, and at the farther end men and boys were
gathering the sheaves into stacks. How could
this be, when yesterday had been September ?
Alongside this field was another field of young
corn, its dark-green stalks not yet tassled out.
Yesterday the ears had been hard as flint, and
long past roasting. I could endure this com-

plication of mysteries no longer. I would stop and consult the men in the carriage behind me. When I stopped, they halted again as before. I started back on foot, leaving my wagon in the road. Seeing this, the carriage came on at a trot until it reached my position, when it slackened to a walk as it reined out to pass me. The two gentlemen stared at me in a most remarkable way, bowed solemnly, and would have passed without a word, if I had not begged them to tell me where the road led to. "The very question we were about to ask you," said the one who held the reins, and then the two exchanged glances. After they had passed me, they threw up the top of the carriage, and I had no doubt they were watching me through the oval window in the back curtain.

I felt a conviction that I must be in the enemy's country. The carriage drove on at a brisk pace, but somehow it never quite disappeared from my view ; or if it did sink into a depression or pass behind a clump of trees, it presently reappeared, going on as before. Once I saw the head of the driver thrust outside the leather top, apparently to speak to a friend who was passing in my direction on foot. The man halted a moment and then came on. He was evidently a young farmer returning from work, for he carried a cradle on his left shoulder, his right hand grasping the back of the scythe-blade which swept diagonally around his right hip. As he approached nearer, I observed with satisfaction that his face wore a pleasant quizzical smile. "Can you tell me," I said, and at the sound of my voice my horse ceased to walk ; "can you tell me where this road leads?"

His smile broadened to a grin ; his right hand left the scythe-blade to tilt his wool hat forward, until I could just see his eyes glitter underneath the brim.

"*When, in the name o' Gord,*" he cried, "*did you come to life, Torm Johnson ?*"

I was staggered at what the man said, but I was more angered at his insolence.

"You haven't answered my question," I roared, half starting from my seat, at which the old horse resumed his walk as if I had spoken to him, and the man, with the same exasperating smile on his face, shouted "Good-by, Torm. The road leads to the river if you go far enough."

I had not thought of myself as Tom Johnson, and yet that was my name. Strange to say, my mind had not gone back of the absorbing events of the battle. I had thus far only considered myself as a convalescent soldier returning to his regiment, which I seemed to have left but yesterday. A longer time must have elapsed, for the seasons had changed —they had even gone backward in the most perplexing way. I passed my fingers again over the tender spot on my head and across the polished surface above.

Tom Johnson! My name came to me like a revelation, as if its familiar sound had not fallen on my ears for ages, and at the same time it connected me with a past to which I wished to return even more than to my regiment. It brought to me the picture of my young wife, standing at the entrance to the drive which led back to our home, and beside her, little Tom crowing in his old mammy's arms. I had fallen out of the dusty ranks to kiss her tearful face and the rosy mouth of baby Tom, and that had been only the day before the battle. Alec, the third, sat erect on the hammer - cloth, holding the reins over the coach-horses behind, and completing the family group. I remembered his familiar voice calling after me :

" Take keer yo'sef, Marse Torm.''

My mind had burrowed back, at last, to the

centre of my world—to the mainspring and motive of my patriotic action. Through the dust of the column, to which I was obliged to return hastily, for we were advancing to give battle to the enemy and straggling was only permitted to those who fell from exhaustion— I waved a last farewell to the group of loved ones whose defence made my service a holy crusade. My State was my country, and my country was the sky above and the earth underneath the feet of that sacred life which had given itself to me, and that other wonderful life to which our lives had given being. I was the defender of a hearthstone, the champion of a gentle mother-spirit, whose innermost thoughts I had shared and whose prayers for my courage and safety were constantly ascending like incense—and of a small unconscious life which, even if I fell, would live on to call my memory blessed.

Where was my regiment? I felt a sort of frenzy to regain that post of duty. What victories had my comrades won in my absence? A sense of shame overcame me that I should be crawling along over that peaceful country road, lulled to indifference by the drowsy influences of the evening—I, the Defender and the Champion!

A child was coming across the field in front of me, but before I had approached near enough to speak to her, she fled back as if I had been some dangerous animal. The carriage, with its mysterious occupants, was still crawling into the distance. The moon was rising on my left, for the sun had already gone down over opposite. The stars were appearing overhead, and a ruddy light illumined the window of a small house by the roadside, to which my weary horse was advancing with the old monotonous walk.

The light from the window lay out on a toll‑bar which spanned the turnpike. I instinctively put my hand in my pocket and drew out a small roll of bills, which looked quite natural and blue in the warm firelight from the doorway. I was about to tender one to the woman who appeared, with a scared look, and extended her hand to the cord which hung from the pulley before the door. "There's nothing to pay," she said. The toll-bar was rising for my passage.

"Where does this road lead, Madam?" I exclaimed, bending eagerly forward to catch her reply.

"I am not to tell you," she said, and the door of the toll-house closed with a bang.

The old horse walked on of his own monotonous will, out of the shadow of the house into
the moonlight. The dry hub creaked and
groaned like a living thing in agony, and the
loose bolts and linchpins jingled in harsh coun-
ter-notes of derision.

I was on the verge of despair. Was all the
world leagued against me? Men, children,
and women avoided me as if I was a leper. I
was Tom Johnson, a highly respectable citizen,
bearing arms in the defence of his country,
hopelessly lost in that or some other country,
where I had as yet seen no soldiers or any
signs of their recent passage or occupancy.
The old horse broke into a gentle trot along
the descending grade, as if it had some intuition
of a camp in advance. Perhaps he was right,
for lights were sparkling among the trees beyond. There was something about the road
which seemed familiar, and yet in many respects it was unlike any road I had ever seen
before. A clump of oaks crowned the knoll
before me, and the walls of a building gleamed
in the moonlight through the tree-trunks. It
was a low, whitewashed church, clean, silent,
deserted. At first I was sure I had been standing in the same place before it yesterday; but
there was no gaping hole above the door as

there had been then, and its walls should be pitted by the iron hail. Even the woods which formed a thick screen behind it had vanished. Was I dreaming? The fields opposite were inclosed with trim, well-kept fences, and the hills were thickly dotted with shocks of newly cut wheat, which perfumed the dewy air with the odor of moist straw. Yes, I must be dreaming. There was a spell of witchery over the land—the stars were not behaving—the moonlight was certainly playing pranks, for above the trees on the highest ground to my left, the gray ghost of a gigantic soldier reared its huge head and shoulders, gleaming and immovable.

I was Tom Johnson, and beyond that everything was disjointed and uncertain. I rubbed my eyes and looked again at the big soldier. There it stood as before, leaning on a gun, and so much as I could see of this figure, or apparition, above the tops of the trees, was as clearly cut against the sky as if it had been carved in stone.

The carriage which had so long preceded me had finally disappeared among the trees where the lights were sparkling. Much as I feared and distrusted its inmates, I felt impelled to follow it as the only moving thing I had to tie

to, and the two men, whether friends or enemies, seemed in some way linked to my helplessness.

Presently I came creaking and jingling into
a village street flanked with stone houses, where
the moonlight broke so fantastically through
the trees, gleaming on white dresses peeping
out of masses of shadow, and mingling with
red lights shining through windows and doors
onto other figures, walking, talking, singing,
laughing, listening to or not heeding the
wheezy notes of a cracked melodeon on one
side of the street and a rioting violin on the
other side—the moonlight everywhere so uncertain, and so bewildering, and so mislead-
ing that the faint sense of familiarity with the
street eluded me like a will-o'-the-wisp ; and
yet, somehow, it seemed that the soldiers had a
right to be there—that the violin should be a
bugle, and that a respectable drum could give
points to that melodeon, and that the long roll
might beat at any moment along that shadowy
street.

As I came creaking and pondering into the
market square, where the line of the houses
was forced a little back to the advantage of the
sidewalks, or rather the flagged plaza into
which those thoroughfares spread out, the moon

poured its unobstructed light onto the gable
end of the very brick building which I had
seen yesterday—(the only yesterday I knew)—
gay with head-quarter flags and glittering uniforms — the turf and flagstones crowded with
restless horses, and a great Confederate banner
floating above the roof.

I was in Sharpsburg.

I leaped out of the wagon and seized my rifle
and coil of blanket. The long tavern stood
opposite, and under the buttonwood-tree which
overspread the rough flagging, a group of men
lounged in chairs and on benches, while a few
others could be seen inside at the dimly lighted
bar.

"When did General Lee leave here?" I
cried, as if I had been summoning the garrison
to surrender. The battle spirit had complete
possession of me for a moment, and the butt of
my gun rang down on the pavement, striking
sparks of fire from the flinty stone.

II

THE carriage which had followed Tom
Johnson's humble outfit out of Hagerstown, passed it on the turnpike, and finally preceded it into Sharpsburg, had contained an eminent surgeon and a physician, well known in
western Maryland. The two medical men had
alighted at the tavern opposite to the red brick
building, which had been Confederate headquarters, and, after greeting the host, had
seated themselves on a bench near the main
entrance, and just out of the radiance of the
oil-lamp which hung over the bar-room door
and shed a ruddy light on the rough flagstones,
even out to the feet of the group of loungers
under the buttonwood - tree. The horse and
carriage had gone around to the stables, and
the reserve of the medical gentlemen had been
respected to that degree that the only evidence
of their presence inhered in two burning stars,
which gleamed from the deep shadow thrown
from the end of the adjoining building, which
stood forward on the line of the street, and in

the fragrant odor of the cigars which the aforesaid medical gentlemen were smoking. The
tavern-keeper, having for the moment no drinks
to mix, stood in his shirt-sleeves in the bar-
room door, and stood also in some obscurity,
as the bottom of the big lamp over his head
was not made of glass, and the light behind
him on the bar was of the dimmest radiance,
and served only to illumine his back. The
cool air of the evening after the heat of the day
had the effect of emptying the grim stone
houses onto the grim stone flagging outside the
doors, under the thick trees where there was
sparse light of an artificial sort, outside of the
rays of moonlight which found their way here
and there through the leafage ; and this was
the drowsy condition of the sleepy old village
when the creaking and jingling outfit of Tom
Johnson came at a snail's pace up the street,
the white horse showing particularly white as
he crossed the occasional patches of moonlight,
and finally came to a stand in the full light between the tavern and the red brick building
over opposite. The peculiar appearance of this
singular visitor sufficiently excited the curiosity
of the villagers to bring men, women, and
children trooping up the street on both sides
to the market square, where they were rapidly

assembling when the butt of Tom's rifle rang down on the pavement and he propounded his startling question. The loungers under the buttonwood-tree stood up in silent amazement, and the circling crowd gazed dumbly at this lonely and belated Confederate soldier standing before them in his gray uniform and dusty equipments.

Tom Johnson looked somewhat dazed as he confronted this formidable assemblage, made more formidable to him by the unwonted presence of so many pretty girls, while at the same time he had good reason to be vexed at the staring crowd and at the absence of any reply to his ringing question.

"What ails you all?" said he, in milder tones than he had at first used, and evidently in deference to the presence of ladies, and then turning to survey the crowd which completely encircled him: "Am I such a curiosity that you can't answer a civil question?"

"You ruther took us by surprise," said the tavern-keeper, who stood in the front rank of the crowd directly confronting Tom.

"You keep this hotel, I reckon," said Tom Johnson, looking straight across into the other's eyes.

"That's so," responded the tavern-keeper, "there's no doubt about that."

"Then please to tell me how long it is since General Lee left this town?" and Tom paused impressively for the expected answer.

"Well, I'll have to figure a little," said the tavern-keeper, scratching his head. "Let me see; it's '92 now. Well, I reckon it'll be thirty years next September since he pulled out o' this town."

Tom Johnson was staggered for a moment by the wildness of the tavern-keeper's mendacity, and then his face flushed several shades redder than it had been in the lamplight.

"You are the most monumental—beg your pardon, ladies," said Tom, glancing around, "I won't say what he is. I reckon he's been drinking too much of his own liquor."

"Where did you come from?" said the tavern-keeper, taking Tom's implication in excellent part.

"I came from hospital," said Tom Johnson, with a shade of helplessness in the tones of his voice.

"What hospital?" said the tavern-keeper.

Tom Johnson was forced to admit that he did not know, and, moreover, he didn't know when or how he came in possession of the horse and wagon which still stood in the road where he had left them. He said that he had

had some trouble with his head, and with that he took off his hat so that the lamplight focussed on his baldness, and ran his fingers absently over the polished surface in search of the soft spot.

" Take that white horse around to the stable," said the tavern-keeper to the hostler, "and lock him up." And then addressing Tom: " Don't you reckon you'd better come in and have somethin' to eat, comrade ? "

Tom Johnson began to feel faint with hunger at the very mention of food, and he was so perplexed and mortified at his inability to account for himself that he was glad of any excuse to escape from the crowd, and so he followed the tavern-keeper into the bar-room, while the villagers surged up to the door and the open windows. He walked directly across to the bar and ran his eye over the bottles.

" Hand me that decanter of brandy," he said, as he leaned his gun against the wall, and ran his fingers once more over his bald head. After he had taken a moderate drink of the liquor diluted with water, he put his hand in his trousers' pocket and produced the roll of blue bills he had taken out at the tollgate, and threw one down on the bar with the evident satisfaction of a man who can at least pay his own way, if he is a little dazed about where he came from.

"What's that?" said the tavern-keeper, picking up the bill and turning it over under the lamp, and then tossing it back. "Is that the kind of money you carry?"

"It's good enough for me," said Tom Johnson, whipping it into his pocket. "I don't carry Federal rags."

The tavern-keeper thrust his hand into his own pocket and drew out a double eagle and rang it down on a copper tray under Tom's nose. "That's the kind o' money we use around here," he said, triumphantly.

Tom Johnson felt of his head, picked up the yellow coin, turned it over in his hand, looked at the face and read the inscription, and then his eye fell on the date. "It's no good," said he. "Look at the date — eighteen hundred and *eighty-three.*"

"That's all right," said the tavern-keeper. "It's nine year old, but it's good, and don't you forget it."

"It's brass," cried Tom Johnson, indignantly, as he threw the coin down on the counter. "I may have been out of my head for quite a while—in the hospital—maybe for weeks, but that's no reason why everybody

should be in a conspiracy to make game of me.
I think you said supper was ready.''

Tom Johnson picked up his gun in view of
the troublous times and followed the tavern-
keeper into the dining-room.

Now, this tavern - keeper had a beautiful
young daughter, with large lustrous eyes and a
complexion like peaches and cream, and as
soon as Tom was comfortably seated at table,
he heard the musical voice of this lovely creature behind him :

'' Would you wish tea or coffee ? ''

'' What ! '' cried Tom. '' Why, coffee, of
course. I haven't tasted coffee in a year,''
and then he turned about until his eye fell on
the sweet girl-face, which blushed red under
his ardent gaze.

'' Pardon me, my dear,'' said Tom, falling
back in his chair and raising his hand to his
head. '' Your daughter,'' he continued, addressing his host, '' reminds me of my young
wife. She's an angel, sir, and God forgive
me, I haven't thought of her or of the baby
since I got out of that wagon. I must leave
here early in the morning. I saw her only a
few days ago when we came this way. Ah, sir,
you should have seen her standing there by the
road and that little rascal, Tom. See here,

old man, you must call me early. I'll find little Tom or the Thirteenth Virginia before night. That's my regiment, the old Thirteenth, and hurrah for old Jack!"

"Why didn't you say you belonged to the Thirteenth before," exclaimed the tavern-keeper. "We've got a Thirteenth man here in town. Do you happen to remember Pete Snavely?"

"Remember Pete!" cried Tom Johnson, pausing for an instant in his eager feeding, "I know him like a brother. We belong to the same company. Wounded?"

"No," said the tavern-keeper, regarding his mysterious guest with a look of wondering compassion; "there's nothing the matter with Pete. Helen," he continued, turning to his daughter, "send around for Pete Snavely, and tell him there's a friend o' his wants to see him."

Pete Snavely needed no sending for, as he had been in the crowd from the first which had welcomed Tom Johnson, and was prominent in the bar-room at that very moment, awaiting the return and discussing the appearance of our hero; and, I am sorry to say, holding very uncomplimentary opinions touching his sanity, and his property relations to the white horse.

Pete was a grizzled old veteran, who had a museum of relics in the basement of the adjoining house, and who, by virtue of his long service as battle-field guide, affected brass buttons and a nondescript uniform, which might suggest both or neither of the old armies. He was so tall that he had to double himself up like a jack-knife when he descended into his curiosity shop, and so lank and lithe that it cost him no trouble to accomplish that feat. Pete Snavely, who stood head and shoulders above the crowd in the bar-room, was engaged in conversation with the doctor and the surgeon, alongside the bagatelle table in the corner, when the tavern-keeper entered, followed by 'Tom Johnson, eager to meet his companion in arms.

"There he is," cried the tavern-keeper, indicating Pete, who stepped briskly forward into the centre of the room. "That's Pete Snavely, of the Thirteenth Virginia."

A shade of disappointment passed over Tom Johnson's face, which was followed by a flush of anger. "What! That old codger? He's old enough to be Pete Snavely's grandfather," and he struck the butt of his gun on the floor and looked Peter over with an expression very much akin to disgust. "He's no comrade of

A Man without a Memory

mine. The Thirteenth Virginia was never accused of robbing the grave for recruits."

Now, Pete was good-natured and, moreover, he believed Tom to be mildly demented, so he smiled blandly at the uncomplimentary speech and surveyed the speaker with a like insolent coolness.

"Well, now, see here, stranger," drawled Pete, at length, "how young do you allow yourself to be?"

"I'm not ashamed of my age," said Tom Johnson. "I'm twenty-three."

"You're about the maturest infant I ever seen," drawled Pete. "Git out o' the way, boys, and let the young gentleman look at himself in the glass."

At this suggestion the crowd stood aside, and Tom Johnson, who had just taken off his hat to pass his hand over his head, and who was carrying his gun at a trail, walked deliberately over to the looking-glass hanging against the wall. Those who stood nearest to him said that his face turned white, at first, at sight of the grizzled and bald-headed image reflected in the mirror, and then he flushed red to the tips of his ears, as with a curse he dashed the glass to atoms with the muzzle of his rifle and staggered back into the arms of Pete Snavely.

32

"Never mind the looking-glass," said the physician, who, with his friend, the surgeon, had been a deeply interested observer of this strange meeting between Tom Johnson as he was and Tom Johnson as he supposed himself to be. "Our patient is a little over-excited," he continued, stepping promptly forward and relieving Pete Snavely of his burden.

Tom Johnson yielded completely to the influence of these men, although he had no recollection of ever having seen them before, except when they had passed him in the carriage on the road. There was something soothing in the touch of the Doctor, and poor Tom, who had been dazed and puzzled and balked at every turn since he had first discovered himself in the wagon, was completely crushed by this last experience. His physical strength seemed to have undergone a complete collapse, until he was like putty in the hands of this strange doctor, whom he obeyed like a child.

"He must go to bed now," said the Doctor, "and have a good night's rest," and to this quiet decision Tom Johnson made no resistance, except to feebly reach for his gun, which had fallen from his grasp in the reaction which followed his ebullition of passion.

The tavern-keeper lighted a candle and led

the way to a chamber, where he remained with the Doctor until Tom was laid safely and comfortably in bed. As the tavern-keeper lingered behind to fetch the candle, Tom rose weakly on his elbow and called after him : " Good-night, old man ; don't forget to call me early in the morning. I want to find her and little Tom."

The Doctor slept in a room adjoining and commanding the only entrance to that of his singular patient, and he took good care that no one should disturb him.

Tom Johnson slept heavily after his strange experience, and when he awoke, with a refreshed and clarified brain, he began, at least, to realize that he was no longer a young man, and to adjust some things, albeit lamely, to that established fact ; for when the Doctor looked in on his patient at sunrise, he found him seated, half-dressed, before a small mirror which stood on a chair, and if his face was not the picture of satisfaction, he showed no disposition to quarrel with the image the glass revealed.

" What does it all mean ? " said Tom, helplessly. " It's a terrible thing to grow old in a single night."

" How old were you on the day you were wounded ? " asked the Doctor, laying his soothing hand on Tom's shoulder.

" I was twenty-three a few days ago, when I was killed," replied Tom, looking steadfastly at the image of the old fellow in the glass.

"And what year was that?" continued the Doctor.

"It was '62," said Tom Johnson.

"And it is '92 this morning," remarked the Doctor, keeping a steady eye on his patient.

" '92 !" exclaimed Tom Johnson, looking hard at the Doctor and making a mental calculation with the aid of his fingers. " '92," he repeated, looking back at his grizzled image in the glass, " that accounts for that old beggar I have been studying since daylight. But for God's sake, Doctor," he exclaimed, springing to his feet, "where have I been in that interval of thirty years ? How old am I now ? Not fifty-three ?"

" Yes, my friend," said the Doctor, laying his hand on his patient's arm, which had the effect of soothing him. " You are fifty-three, and during that long interval, dating from the day and hour when you received your wound on this field, *You have been a man without a memory*. During all that time your life has been to yourself a blank, and I must tell you at once that you owe your restoration to the skill of that great surgeon whom you saw in my company yesterday. Be calm and listen. But for his skill, which has relieved your brain from the pressure of the misplaced bone, and whose watchful care, through fever and unconscious suffering, has brought you quietly back to this scene of your injury, your life would still be a blank.''

Tom Johnson gazed speechless into the Doctor's face as he made this amazing statement, and then his unconscious hand stole softly to his head.

The Doctor forbore to break the silence, holding his patient under his kindly gaze.

'' Praise God ! '' exclaimed Tom Johnson at last, rising and grasping the Doctor's hands. '' You have brought me back to life. You have rescued me from a living grave—Praise God ! But where have I been, Doctor, during all these years ? ''

'' With your family at your old home, surrounded with every comfort——''

'' Have mercy, Doctor,'' exclaimed Tom Johnson, staggering. '' Don't trifle with me.''

'' You forget,'' said the Doctor, waving his patient back into his chair, ''*that you were a man without a memory.*''

'' And I was really there with her and little Tom ? How is that precious baby, Tom ?

Tell me quick, Doctor,'' and he was on his feet again, reaching for his old gray uniform coat.

" He is in China just now,'' replied the Doctor.

"What ?'' roared Tom Johnson, with one arm in the sleeve of his coat.

" He is Lieutenant-Commander Johnson, of the navy,'' said the Doctor.

"What ! That baby !'' cried Tom. " An officer in the navy ! Hurrah ! I'm glad to hear he is serving his country. How did he get there ? ''

" In the usual way,'' said the Doctor. " You sent him to the Naval Academy and paid his bills, or rather your money did.''

" Good,'' said Tom Johnson, who still stood before the Doctor, with his old coat half on. " I believe everything you tell me. Would to God I had another boy to give to the same service.''

" You have,'' said the Doctor, " and he is also in the navy.''

Tom Johnson stared at the Doctor without opening his lips, and when he was about to speak he was restrained by a warning finger. " You are about to forget again that you have been a man without a memory.''

Tom stood in silence for a moment, the better to grasp the surprising information, his coat still dangling from one shoulder, and then he raised his free arm above his head. "Thank God," he exclaimed, fervently, "that I have two sons in the service of the Confederacy, and she—she——"

He had seized both hands of the Doctor, and was trembling visibly as he breathlessly awaited a reply.

For the first time the Doctor was silent.

"My wife — my darling — where is she?" and as he put these questions passionately, Tom Johnson clung desperately to the strong white hands of the man he trusted, he knew not why.

"God have mercy on him," ejaculated the Doctor, fervently. "*He has been a man without a memory.*"

"Dead! Dead!" groaned Tom Johnson, dropping the Doctor's hands, and seating himself on the bed. "Oh, why did you bring me back to life?"

The Doctor sat down beside his patient and put an arm about his shoulders to soothe him as best he could. "It was years ago, my dear fellow," he began. "She was a good wife to you, and you lived long together in a happy home. She anticipated your every want. You lived a half-conscious life without any recognition of the past. Your infirmity was the only cross she had to bear. You were constantly with her in her last sickness. You closed her eyes with your own hands, and you have often stood by her grave, where the sunset stretches its golden bars under the dark pines. Not that you knew why you were there, but she entreated Tom with her last breath to bring you to her often, and her one hope and prayer was that some day you might come understanding why you came." The Doctor ceased speaking.

"Leave me alone for a while," said his stricken patient, who was overcome by this first knowledge of his bereavement, just as if he were standing by the dead form of his beloved wife, who had at that moment ceased to breathe.

Tom Johnson kept his room and would see no one during that day, even refusing the food that was offered him; but with the dawn of another morning he called for his old comrade in arms, Pete Snavely, of the Thirteenth Virginia. When the latter appeared, towering in the doorway, the two literally fell into each other's arms, with voluble protestations and explanations and apologies, for Pete had had no idea at the time the looking-glass had been smashed in the bar-room that he had been chaffering little Tom Johnson, of the old Thirteenth.

"Tommy," blubbered Pete, as he held his comrade to his breast, clad in the sacred old uniform which now moved him to tears, "it's all over what we fit for."

Tom Johnson released himself from the embrace of the weeping giant, and looked up at him with a terrified expression. "You mean the war's over, Pete," he said, feebly grasping at this interpretation of his comrade's meaning.

"No, I don't," whimpered Pete, determined to have the worst over with the least delay. "I mean the Confederacy was busted, turned down more'n a quarter of a century ago—snuffed out like you was, Tommy, under that old thorn-tree—the niggers was set free, everybody nigh about was killed—but by G—, Tommy, the way we fit ag'in odds was a thing to be everlastin'ly proud of."

Tom Johnson had fallen back to a sitting position on the edge of the bed, his face of an ashen pallor, which frightened his comrade to see. Pete Snavely partially shut himself up and deposited his knife-ship on a chair over opposite. "Never mind, Tommy," he said, wiping his eyes; "it's all ancient history now, and we did our level best with bibles in our pockets and tooth-brushes in our button-holes. The difference between Blue-bellies and Gray-backs don't count no mo', and the fact is, Tommy, we're all Yankees now, and rather proud of it."

This unwelcome news coming so suddenly was utterly appalling and crushing in its effect on Tom Johnson, particularly when he realized that baby Tom and the son he had no recollection of ever having seen, were actually serving under the despised Yankee flag. It made him angry to think that he himself had been living under its folds for an ordinary life time, unconscious and unprotesting, as if an unfair advantage had been taken of his peculiar condition, which amounted to a personal affront. It was a positive relief to him to learn that his beloved old commander, Stonewall Jackson, had fallen in the fore front of battle, and had thus been spared the humiliation of conscious defeat.

"Don't take it to heart so, Tommy," said Pete, shrugging his shoulders and turning out the palms of his hands. "There ain't so many o' we all left, and the kids that's been born since the war, in one State o' the forty-four,

could drive both o' the old armies into the sea.
We're back numbers, Tommy, that's what we
are.''

"I'm afraid so," said Tom Johnson, standing up and readjusting his belt over his old
gray coat. "I shan't need this gun any
more," he remarked, sadly, as he drew the
iron ramrod and rang it down in the empty
barrel. "Somebody has drawn the charge."

Peter Snavely, who had some new surprise
every hour for his old comrade in arms, took him
under his protecting wing, and the latter gradually put off his rusty equipments, exchanging his
old uniform for a respectable suit of sober gray
cloth, and it was quite refreshing to see him
thus transformed by dainty linen and clean
shaving, et cetera, into a courtly old gentleman
with good money in his pocket, and a gold
chronometer on his fob ; in short, put back externally in the well-groomed condition his body
had been accustomed to before he came under
the hands of the surgeon, with the addition of
a brain as clear as the tone of a Japanese gong.

The two were always together (the one short
and sturdy, and the other lank and tall, as that
President Lincoln, of whom Tom had had but
a poor opinion), except when Mr. Thomas
Johnson disappeared for a few days to look

over his property and stand by the grave of
that wife who had stood bravely and lovingly
beside him during so many years when he had
been a man without a memory.

His home had no attraction for him, to be
compared with the claims of his old comrade,
and so he preferred to surround himself with
such comforts as he could at the long tavern
under the buttonwood-tree over opposite the old
head-quarters, where he could enjoy his pipe
and his glass with Pete Snavely, of the old
Thirteenth, and walk out at will to the knotted
and deformed thorn-tree which still overhung
the fenceless gash in the fields known as the
bloody lane.

One day in September, namely, the fifteenth,
in the year of our Lord, 1892, a letter arrived
at the Sharpsburg office addressed to '' Thomas
Johnson, Esquire,'' and post-marked ''Newport News.'' Pete Snavely clasped and unclasped himself with more agility than usual,
as he descended the stone steps into the basement museum where his old comrade was
smoking his pipe, among the glass cases of
shells and canteens and buttons and oxidized
bullets, in an environment bristling with guns
and sabres and rusty lances of the John Brown
period. The letter was signed '' Baby Tom,''

who had steamed into port from the Chinese seas, a full Captain in the Navy under orders to report at the navy yard at Washington, whence he was to proceed to New York to take command of the new ram Constitution, where he would be granted leave to come and embrace his dear old father, in his joyful restoration.

Tom Johnson, Sr., wiped the moisture from his eye-glasses, and with a promptness born of his military training ordered Pete Snavely to pack his knapsack forthwith. " Put in your Sunday clothes and plenty of them," cried Tom Johnson, and the tall comrade had come so completely under the control of the short one who carried the check - book that he obeyed without a question, and the two old soldiers were seated under the buttonwood-tree when the carriage came up for the station.

They had a couple of hours at Hagerstown before the night train, and in all probability Captain Johnson, U. S. N., was then at the Washington navy yard. When Pete Snavely's eye fell on a long-distance telephone in the hotel office, he bribed the clerk to call up the Commandant's quarters and, sure enough, Captain Johnson was there, whom Pete informed of the presence of his father and requested him to stop at the instrument.

"Come this way, Tommy," roared Pete; "there's a man outside wants to speak to you on the telephone."

Tom Johnson came, but he had never seen or heard of a telephone, having been quite busy enough during the last two months catching up with other things. It was a sort of new-fangled telegraph, Pete said, and showed him how to put the receiver to his ear. Tom Johnson handled it very much as if it were loaded, and started a little when the bell rang; but he followed Pete's instructions and called "Hello!"

"Why, it echoes back in this thing," exclaimed Tom.

"Now, does it?" said Pete, pushing the receiver back to his ear. "That's the other fellow a hundred miles from here. Tell him you are Tom Johnson and ask him who he is."

The most surprising answer came back, which caused the old man in gray to drop the receiver and feel for the soft spot on the top of his head, after the pleasant way he had of expressing perplexity and surprise.

"He says he's Baby Tom, from China!"

"Well, I reckon he ought to know, Tommy," said Pete Snavely. "He's eatin' fried chicken with the Admiral in Washington this minute, and you better ask him for a drum-stick."

So it fell out that father and son had a meeting at long range, in which everything was fixed, and it is certain that no telephone before or since has ever heard such eager " helloes " and affectionate " good-byes " as passed each other on that happy occasion ; and in consequence thereof the Captain's launch with the Captain in it met the two old soldiers at the landing, and Baby Tom looked so tall and bronzed and smart in his glittering uniform that his old daddy was overcome with awe and admiration for a sixth of a minute before the two came to close quarters, to all of which Pete Snavely can testify, for he clasped and unclasped himself during the functions and amenities incident to this meeting between father and son with a rapidity that suggested a dancing-jack.

During all this time the new Constitution, toward which the copper - coated launch was presently dancing over the swells, lay out in the river and in the sunlight, dressed in bunting from stem to stern, with four hundred pairs of canvas trousers and four hundred shirts fluttering from the stays ; and the deck was manned to receive the new Commander and his guests, and the little old man in gray was sufficiently impressed with the dignity and importance of " Baby Tom."

During their stay on board and their pere-
grinations on shore these two old veterans saw
more of the world and the sea than they had
ever dreamed of before, and they dined in such
state with the Commander that they found
themselves drinking bumpers to the flag before
they knew it. They looked through the winding, oily bore of the ten - inch rifle which
ranged over the nickel-steel prow of the ram,
and found the whole wonderful interior of the
ship crowded here and there as compactly
with delicate machinery as the case of a watch,
and when they found themselves back at the
long tavern under the buttonwood - tree, with
the Captain in their company, they couldn't
forget the wonders they had seen or divest
themselves of the loyalty they had unconsciously put on.

When Tom Johnson asked the Captain, his
son, if the Constitution couldn't sink any bat-
tle-ship or any other ship afloat, the Captain
said he thought it might, but next year every
battle - ship would carry sufficient dynamite
tubes, for use at short range, to blow him up
in a white cloud at just fifty yards short of the
fatal impact ; and then he confided to his
father that the steel monsters of the day were
at heart the most arrant hypocrites and mission-

aries of peace, and that their commanders
everywhere had such a profound and growing
respect for each other, that he had to laugh
into his cocked hat sometimes to think of it.
The Captain told them, moreover, as they
smoked their pipes under the buttonwood-tree,
that in a few years the naval attacks would all
be made under water, while the officers of the
directing battle-ships were drinking champagne
and watching each other through powerful
glasses, and that in the end all naval combats
would be decided by mathematical computa-
tions made by the Admirals on shore, to which
the tavern - keeper, who had been born since
the battle, said that things were certainly coming to a pretty pass.

In due time, after father and son had stood
together by the grave under the pines, and
talked much of the absent son and brother,
the Captain went away to join his ship, and
things settled down to a normal condition at
the long tavern under the buttonwood - tree.
The two old comrades, the long one and the
short one, may still be seen wandering about
the historic field, and Tom Johnson has a new
respect for the countless dead in the Government cemetery, and a positive affection for
the big stone soldier standing silent guard

above them (which he had mistaken for a ghost in the moonlight as he came crawling back into Sharpsburg in the creaking outfit, behind the old gray horse), and which, leaning on its stone gun, looks complacently out over the tree-tops across the smiling wheat-fields to the whitewashed walls of the low Dunker church and the sunlit strip of turnpike, where the battle raged so fiercely.

The Wedding Journey of Mrs. Zaintree (Born Greenleaf)

THE WEDDING JOURNEY OF MRS. ZAINTREE (BORN GREENLEAF)

I

QUITE the greatest surprise that had ever been meted out to the fastidious members of the Peter Stuyvesant Club (limited) befell when the news came of the marriage of Colonel Zaintree to a lady of suitable age and accomplishments, whom, rumor said, he had met in Norway, where both parties to the inevitable had been engaged in the innocent pursuit of the midnight sun. That so eccentric a member of a close corporation of bachelors should do such a commonplace thing, under the vulgar cloak of secrecy, which involved a hasty return across the Atlantic and the successful avoidance of his friends, was regarded by Major Cavendish and his right and left hand adversaries of the Colonel's particular table as nothing less than a tricky finesse.

In addition to the concise and correct announcement of the names of the two high contracting parties in an evening journal, there followed the surprising statement that :

" The groom wore a ten-button frock coat of American broadcloth, with a boutonnière of golden nasturtiums on the left lapel ; a turn-down linen collar, silver-gray trousers, creased, with gloves to match, and carried in his hand a stick of Irish blackthorn, the gift of the bride."

Both the Colonel and Mrs. Zaintree had spent many summers in Europe, during which sojourns (in severalty) they had explored that eminently respectable continent both along and beyond the ordinary itinerancy. Both had listened to the thunder of Niagara ; the lady had visited the wonders of the Yosemite and the old Spanish Missions of Southern California, and the Colonel harbored some unpleasant recollections of the Great Geyser basin in the Yellowstone National Park. He had, in fact, cut his name in the soft clay of one of the minor basins, contrary to the Government keep-off-the-grass regulations ; and to make a salutary example of him, the officer in charge had telegraphed the fact to the captain of cavalry at the entrance, and the Colonel had been obliged to travel one hundred and sixty miles by stage to erase his signature.

Barring these points, and the railways necessary to reach them, and not taking into account some geographical knowledge the Colonel had picked up with the Army of the Potomac, their own country, outside of a tiny circle which should include Newport and Tuxedo, was a wide terra incognita.

If the Colonel was bent on anything it was on making a unique wedding journey in the by-ways of travel, by unaccustomed means of transportation, leading to nowhere in particular, with necessarily no feverish anxiety on the part of the travellers to get there. With money in his purse and a check-book in his breast-pocket, and the hearty approval of the angel at his side, they were off for a romp in the dark, and about the whole strange business there was a delightful uncertainty, which was in itself a pretty satire on the element of uncertainty connected with the longer journey upon which they were making simultaneous entry with such light hearts and high hopes.

Of course they had to get out of town in an ordinary vestibule train, with its dreary, glittering vista of polished mahogany fittings, broken by staring silver-plated ornaments, monogram glass, nice-enough china dinner-service, ebony waiters in spotless linen, and the endless procession of respectables and fashionables, coming and going, reading papers, cutting the leaves of new books, and travelling-caps talking offensive politics with mysterious double eye-glasses. The Colonel tweaked his gray mustache and swore inwardly there should be an end of it, and Madam composed her gloved hands and just perceptibly shrugged her well-bred shoulders that there should be so many observers of her happiness and withal such a wilderness of respectable indifference to it.

After a dainty breakfast of golden melon with water-cress, the freshest of rolls, and the most fragrant of coffee, served on a little table between the high-backed seats in their own particular domain, the Colonel tore himself away from his domestic happiness and walked forward to enjoy his cigar and his morning paper. Instead of stopping in the first smoking-compartment, he strolled on through car after car until he found a seat to his liking, and settling himself comfortably before a window, he was straightway lost in contemplation of the running landscape flooded with the sunlight of his own happiness. He forgot his morning paper, and even the small brown Havana hung unlighted between his listless fingers. His misspent life was before him, and the bachelor friends of his club, in their unsuspected misery, were jumbled with the fences and the trees, and the clouds were taking the shape of some of the girls he remembered. He was as far from them all and pitied them as much as if he had suddenly become the emperor of a continent in Mars.

Presently he bethought himself of his cigar, without forgetting his happiness, and struck a match on the iron fire-dogs in the hall of the Peter Stuyvesant.

" Hello, Zaintree, going to Chicago ? "

The Colonel fell out of the clouds like a collapsed balloon, with an indistinct feeling that he had been engaged in something reprehensible.

" Nothing gone wrong, I hope," said the other— " drop in exchange or slump in cotton ? "

" Not a bit of it, Ketcham," cried the Colonel, shaking his friend warmly by the hand. " Something has gone overwhelmingly right, and, to tell you an open secret, I have been getting married."

" Well, you're old enough. I congratulate you. Tickets for Sitka ? "

" Not quite so bad as that," said the Colonel. " The tickets are nominally for Buffalo, but I can't promise you we shall not get off before we reach there and take a wagon across

country. I beg you will be seated," continued
the Colonel, laying open his cigar-case, "and
after we have talked the matter over let me
have the pleasure of presenting an old friend to
Mrs. Zaintree. Certainly, Ketcham, you are
about the last man I expected to find ashore in
these sweltering days."

"If it's yachting you mean, Colonel, I have
given it up for family reasons," said the gentleman of the name of Ketcham, who was of about
the Colonel's age, having a smooth-shaven face,
large hearty Western ways, and something indescribable in his manner that hinted of soft
winds blowing over many lands. "Wives have
their limitations, Colonel," continued Commodore Ketcham. "Mine was launched without
sea-legs, and when a captain's first mate spends
the best part of the cruise in the seclusion of
the cabin, it's time to go ashore and stay
there."

"Naturally," mused the Colonel.

"So the Happy Thought is dismantled and
laid up indefinitely. I'm sorry for it too, Colonel; if she was in commission this minute I
would put her at your disposal for a honeymoon
cruise," and the ex-Commodore of the Buffalo
Yacht Club laid one hand regretfully on the
Colonel's knee and snapped the fingers of the

other in vexation at his sheer inability to do the handsome thing.

The Colonel, who understood his friend thoroughly, expressed his regrets briefly and feelingly, knowing that the situation annoyed the Commodore like a belated thought haunting the memory of an after-dinner speech.

The two gentlemen now cast aside their cigars and took their way down the train, the Colonel with a comfortable pride in a new and inestimable possession, and the Commodore conscious of an agreeable curiosity and a personal solicitude concerning first impressions.

An hour later the train was running smoothly over the rails among the scattered homes of the laborers and market-gardeners on the outskirts of Rochester, the Commodore seated opposite to the bride with a comfortable feeling that he had known and admired her indefinitely, and a keen regret that circumstances over which he had no control were about to separate old friends and new.

Mrs. Zaintree was saying the thousand and one cordial things which a well-bred and kind-hearted lady knows so well how to say: " The Colonel's friends were her friends. The Commodore must certainly dine with them on his

very earliest visit to New York, and she should
take good care to find out his favorite dish
before he came. She looked forward to the
pleasure of knowing his wife, who was no sailor,
and it was so sweet of him to give up the water
for her sake.''

"My dear Mrs. Zaintree," said the Commodore, " to be exact, I have given it up with
a reservation. That is to say, the down-town
house of Self & Co. has fitted up a couple of
cabins, fore and aft, on the iron freighter Nautilus, and I go aboard sometimes for a cruise on
the lake, with a friend or two. A basket of
wine and a few brace of ducks in the larder,
and a quiet rubber in the cabin. You understand, Colonel?''

" Why, look here," cried the Colonel, "that
eclipses the idea of the yacht.''

"It's ever so much jollier," exclaimed Mrs.
Zaintree. " Do you know, I sailed on a Dutch
lugger with fins, like a great fish, from Rotterdam to Ymuiden in the North Sea, with a little
party of English and Americans last year, and
it was the nicest trip of the whole summer.''

" But my vessel is loaded with coal.''

" And the Dutch fin-boat carried fish.''

" Where is the Nautilus bound?'' asked the
Colonel.

"There it is again," said the Commodore; "unfortunately I haven't the remotest idea. She may be booked for Cleveland, or she may be for Three Mile Harbor, or any other port on the Lakes. The deck-hands swear all day and play the accordion all night. Cook cuts the beef in cubes——"

"Just like the Rotterdam lugger," broke in the lady, with enthusiasm, "and sailing with sealed orders too. Not another word, Commodore, in disparagement of the Nautilus. Anything that is good enough for Commodore Ketcham and his friends is good enough for us."

"Precisely so," said the Colonel. "Put us on board the Nautilus by all means, if our presence will be no hindrance to the business of the vessel."

"Not an atom," cried the Commodore, whose hand was already on his travelling-bag, with none too much time to make his Southbound train. "I'll telegraph the office to hold her until you come, and you must stop in the waiting-room of the station, like two orphans, until you are called for. I shall write the telegram in the carriage going across town, and Captain Webb and the cook will pipe you over the side in royal style. Tut, tut, not a

word, and not an anxious thought for your-
selves or your luggage, and good-by, and good-
by, and a pleasant cruise," and the Commodore
hurried away with the outgoing crowd.

It naturally occurred to Mrs. Zaintree, as the
Commodore was disappearing, that it would be
as well to conceal the fact of their recent marriage from the profane and musical deck-hands,
and with that modest end in view she hurried
the Colonel off in pursuit, who was just in time
to buttonhole his friend as he was stepping into
a carriage.

"You sly dog," laughed the Commodore,
squeezing the Colonel's hand, "I was a young
man myself once. I'll telegraph the Captain
that you expect your eldest son to come on
board at Detroit."

The Colonel stood an inch higher in his own
estimation as the carriage containing the Commodore rattled off over the stones. Mrs. Zaintree saw something outside the window that
claimed her attention for a moment, and then
she commended the Commodore's cleverness,
and intimated that if they should not pass Detroit it would be a grave disappointment to the
supposititious young man.

The July sun, climbing up into a cloudless
sky, promised a day of unusual heat, and the

long train had become twice as stuffy as before
since the cruise on the lake had been decided
on.

" It will be just like the Dutch lugger," said
the lady, " only a great deal nicer.   Instead of
fishy planks the cabin-floor will be spread with
white sand, and we can walk around the coal,
and I am sure there will be no great patches on
the Commodore's sails, and the Captain will let
me take a turn at the wheel, and we will imagine Lake Erie is the North Sea, and only think
of it, you darling Colonel, we don't know where
we are going."

The hot fragrance of the clover came in at
the open window.   The cool green of the corn
overspread the gently rolling hills, away to the
purple woods, and laughed in the face of the
shimmering heat.   The towns and the orchards
slid by, and the long western - bound freight
trains seemed to stand still, with a ridiculous
make-believe of flurry and steam, for the flying
express to pass.

The Colonel felt assured that the will of the
Commodore was already working wonders in
their behalf in the city by the lake.   And so it
turned out, for the carriage that picked them
up at the station was already half-loaded with
wicker-baskets and hampers, and the handsome

assistant - engineer on the box knew all about them, and had anticipated all their wants just as if they had been expected for a month.

It was nothing that they had to mount a rickety ladder, and cross the deck of a schooner, whose greasy cook - shop was redolent of onions, and whose seamy sides smelt of tar and bilge - water. Another ladder rose from the offensive deck against a wall of iron, and the bronze smile of Captain Webb of the Nautilus was beaming a welcome from the top.

Madam the cook, in a clean white apron, with her keys in a basket, led them up the long deck to their quarters in the forecastle; and Wilhelm, her husband and first assistant, his bald head sparkling in the sun like the ship's binnacle, brought up the rear, to lend a hand in stowing the luggage, which was neatly piled outside a pretty white door, the formidable pyramid crowned with the Colonel's hat-box.

"THE dear old Commodore!" thought Mrs. Zaintree, sweeping the polished decks with the comprehensive eye of an experienced globe-trotter, "it was all a fib about the coal." If the exclusive passengers of the Nautilus were pleased with the external appearance of the craft, its trim smoke-stacks crowned with a billow of scintillating heat from the suppressed energy below, what were their surprise and delight at the revelation of comfort and luxury that lay behind the little white door by the pyramid of luggage.

A darkened vista of cabins, two in number, panelled with sycamore and half-separated with silken draperies, and an opposite door opening on a well-appointed bath-room. A velvet carpet under foot; a white-curtained bed beyond the dividing drapery; great easy-chairs and couches backed with carved dolphins and upholstered in leather; glittering lamps hanging from the ceilings; a dainty writing-table hooked to the wall under the window looking on the deck; two other curtained windows overlook-

ing the tarry bowsprit of the schooner alongside, and a little shelf of new novels with uncut
leaves. A winding staircase led up to the Captain's quarters above, and so out onto the short
upper deck where the watch alternated before
the glazed wheel-house.

"It's not a bit like the Dutch lugger with
red fins," said the bride, out of a nest of
cushions, "any more than little Holland is like
big America, thanks to the charming taste of
the Commodore."

There was a gentle throb in the timbers of
the Nautilus, the tarry ropes had disappeared
from the open windows, and a little stir of
fresher air fluttered the curtains; a deluge of
cool water from some mysterious source streamed
over the cabins and presently spluttered and
dashed against the door and window inboard,
and when the forward cabins had received a
satisfactory cleansing externally, the man with
the hose turned his attention to the main-deck,
and Colonel and Mrs. Zaintree, bound nowhere
in particular, so far as they yet knew, were well
out on the blue waters of Lake Erie, the black
smoke billowing and tumbling from the twin
stacks away aft with something mysterious about
it, like the far-reaching hospitality of the Commodore.

It was quite a wonderful ship, the Nautilus, for a carrier of freight, and the coal was really battened down under the hatches, a full cargo of it. More than half of her length was clean unencumbered deck, stretching between the cabins fore and aft, protected by low bulwarks and dominated by two tall masts without a thread of canvas; and this timber paddock lay in front of the Colonel's door, so that once out of sight of land, where the cool winds tempered the warmth of the sun, the fortunate couple found it a delightful promenade whereon to saunter up and down, encased in warm flannels.

Indeed it was quite a respectable walk to and from the dining-cabin, where the cook's green-and-gold parrot chose the nick of time in which to scream, " Make way for the Captain.'' In the little state cabin aft, alongside the main dining-room, a round table was laid with two covers for the Commodore's guests, and with a third, by request of the Colonel, for the use of the Captain whenever he was at liberty to join them. The Nautilus's monogram silver came out of its glass - case, and the private lockers yielded of their store of dainty linen and china to grace this extra board.

At supper, on the very first day out, Captain

Webb, who had gone to the extra length of putting on his coat for the occasion, which staggered the parrot, eying him through the open door, into utter silence, announced that the steamer would pass up the Detroit River the next evening, where young Mr. Zaintree would come out in the reporter's boat.

"Long since you have seen your son, ma'am?" asked the Captain.

Mrs. Zaintree said it was a long time, and the Colonel hastened to add that Jack was not very reliable, and he shouldn't be surprised to see the boat come alongside without him.

"Never fear, ma'am," said the Captain, with an effort at gallantry, which had about it a flavor of the Commodore's wine, "if your son esteems his charming mother as she deserves, and he wouldn't be the Colonel's boy if he didn't, we shall hook him up with the evening papers. Dear me, no," continued the Captain, "the boat never stops, she just slows down a bit and we lower a ladder. Of course, ma'am, he will sleep in this cabin, it is all we have to offer him; but the more the merrier, Colonel, and it's all in the family. If you should conclude, ma'am, that you would rather have him on one of the sofas in your quarters, the cook will fix him comfortable. If you don't own the boat this trip I don't know who does,'' and the Captain closed the outer door behind him and went whistling away to his watch.

The Colonel and his bride laughed merrily at the huge success of the Commodore's telegram. They looked down at the grimy stokers, feeding the furnaces, and made a descent into the moist, warm atmosphere of the engine-room, where the great oily giant of propulsion was doing its mysterious, noiseless work, with a ceaseless gliding of steel bars, flecked with little heart-beats of thin steam from the joints of the monster's glittering brass-mounted harness.

The engineer was so polite to the Commodore's guests and so proud of his machinery, and the atmosphere of the ship-wide room was so balmy, with its pretty writing - desk in the corner, and the green water rushing by the open ports, and the curious dial on the engine, that dropped an additional black figure for every revolution of the shaft (and had been dropping figures ceaselessly from the very start up into the hundred thousands)—these things were all so interesting and so marvellous that the oleaginous odor of the place became a rather pleasant perfume, so that when they went out the chill of the evening on deck was sharpened by comparison.

The steam was turned on in the radiators in the forward cabins, and the lamps alight, but the night was so fine outside that our travellers went up to join the Captain's watch in front of the wheel-house.

. . . .

It was perhaps four o'clock in the afternoon of the second day of the cruise when the Nautilus was steaming up past the forts and the big straw-colored Exhibition building, relieved against the canopy of smoke which overhung the city of Detroit, spreading back from the flat level of the river.

The Colonel was eager to get the papers, and Mrs. Zaintree was plying the Captain with questions about every prominent object on either shore, going from side to side of the bow, coming into collision with the capstan on the way to Canada, and running against the binnacle on the Michigan side, and manifesting less interest in her offspring, the Captain thought, than a she-bear would show for her cub. It rather annoyed the Captain to think so. In many respects Mrs. Zaintree was the most accomplished woman Captain Webb had ever come in contact with. In his private log he had entered

her as "a thoroughbred." Her perfect self-
possession seemed to him like an invisible armor
through which her frank, cordial manner and
engaging womanly ways shone like a soft, warm
light. Her low modulated voice struck on his
ear like music. In every other respect the
Colonel's wife was altogether lovely, but her
conduct as a mother completely staggered his
reckoning.

If the lady divined, to some extent, what
was passing in the Captain's mind, she was too
honest to dissemble unnecessarily, and a few
unavoidable expressions of regret for the non-
appearance of the mythical Jack, after Detroit
should be left behind, would make it all right.
When she restored him his glass, with a pretty
speech of thanks for his kindness, and disappeared down the companion-way, and that just
before he got the first view of the reporter's
boat pushing out from the shore, the Captain
shook his head and pondered on the mysterious
ways of womankind.

At the same moment that these perplexing
thoughts were vexing the Captain's brain, Mr.
Jack Dorr, of Toledo, O., seated in the stern
of the newsman's boat, had his eye on the Nautilus steaming up the river. He was speculat-

ing as to how his four dogs and all his hunting traps and personal luggage could be safely got over the side of the steamer, which was totally oblivious of his existence and wouldn't have stopped for the Commodore himself. But Mr. Jack Dorr had an authorization from the Toledo office, duly signed and sealed, to board the Nautilus as she passed Detroit, and his serenity was not in the least disturbed by the difficulty the officers would encounter in making the transfer of himself and his effects. That was their business he flattered himself, and he was only conscious of an amused curiosity as to how they would acquit themselves in the emergency he was about to thrust upon them.

"The Nautilus is a slowin' up for somethin'," the boatman observed, as he stuffed a bundle of newspapers into a tin pail, with a line attached to the pail. Mr. Jack Dorr observed for himself that a ladder was already over the side, and instead of holding up the potent document as he had fully intended to do, he threw away his cigar, and administered a corrective cuff apiece to two restive young hounds who showed signs of disturbing the dignity of his establishment with their uncalled-for music. "That must be the skipper," he thought, as he complacently took in the authoritative figure of Captain Webb, making the boat's line fast to a thole-pin.

"Don't disturb yourself, Mr. Zaintree," shouted the authoritative figure at the rail, "until we get the dogs on board."

Mr. Jack Dorr had not the slightest intention of disturbing himself. It was not his way. He had been agreeably surprised by the abundant evidence that he, or somebody else, was expected to board the vessel at this particular point, and the Captain, himself, addressing him by the unheard-of name of Zaintree, gave a fresh and pleasing interest to the mystery.

"Look here, John," said Mr. Jack Dorr, from his seat in the stern, naming the newsman at random, "take that liver-and-white setter under your arm, and drop her on board; see? Don't be afraid of her, man. It's all right, skipper, my dogs are up to this sort o' thing."

When the boatman came down for the last dog he brought the surprising information that his passenger's father and mother were on board.

"The devil you say," said Mr. Jack Dorr. "I'm glad to know it."

"Old folks all right, skipper?" cried Jack,

at last, with a hearty grasp of the Captain's hand that won the sailor's heart by storm. "They don't appear to be dying to see their son."

"Your reckoning is about right," said Captain Webb, taking no care to conceal the double meaning of his words. "There comes the *Colonel* now."

Mr. Jack Dorr took in his new parent at a glance — a glance of satisfied approval, and hastened across the deck to meet him.

"Glad to see you, governor! Never saw you looking better!" And there was an amused twinkle of inquiry in Jack's eyes as he looked straight across into the Colonel's.

The Colonel was taken altogether by surprise, for he had been reading in the cabin, and came out with the expectation of encountering nothing more personal than the editorial thrusts in the Detroit papers, and when he saw Jack greeting the Captain, he suspected that the Commodore had put off a practical joke on him, and he concluded to accept the situation philosophically. The Colonel was a sensitive man, and it was no part of his plan to be made the laughing-stock of the crew, so he returned the strange young man's greeting heartily enough, and the two turned away in the direction of the forecastle.

"You mustn't mind my calling you governor," said Jack. "As the boys say, 'Everything goes when you're away from home.' The Captain called me Zaintree, or Braintree, over the rail, and sent me word that my father and mother were on board, and I accepted the situation, pop, just as I found it."

"The Captain called you Zaintree, did he?" said the Colonel with a smile. "What does the Commodore call you?"

"If you mean Commodore Ketcham," said Jack, "I don't know him from a side of sole leather, but here is my card. You are Colonel Zaintree, I presume, and as for myself, the surprising events that have occurred since I came alongside this ship leave me in something of a fog as to who I am."

The Colonel put on his gold eye-glasses and read the very correct social statement :

Mr. John Dorr.

"Hum," mused the Colonel, "then you don't know the Commodore, Mr. Dorr?"

"I haven't the pleasure," said Jack. "And by the way, governor, if our relationship is to go on this trip, you had better forget my name altogether and call me plain Jack."

Colonel Zaintree pondered the situation in

silence for a moment, during which he ran a quick eye over the irreproachable exterior of the young man who had accosted him so breezily. The disagreeable alternative of renouncing the relationship already publicly assumed, the Colonel wisely decided, had best be submitted to the judgment of the third party interested.

Captain Webb saw the gentlemen disappear through the little white door with regret, for the singular maternal conduct of the otherwise admirable Mrs. Zaintree was still vexing his mind, and he had hoped to be a witness of such a cordial meeting with her son as should triumphantly vindicate her character as a mother.

When, however, a half-hour afterward, he looked down from the bridge and saw the three pacing the deck arm in arm, the lady addressing the greater part of her conversation to Jack, he thought it a very pretty family tableau, and privately voted himself a fool for his suspicions.

If he had seen the meeting in the cabin, without hearing the words that were spoken, he would have been equally satisfied with Mrs. Zaintree's conduct as a high-bred mother and with Jack's behavior as a dutiful son. The set speech of the Colonel in presenting the young gentleman died on his lips, half uttered, as he saw his wife drop the book she had been reading and advance with both hands extended, her face beaming with a smile of welcome and uttering the one word, "*Jack !*"

As for Mr. Jack Dorr, he came as near being surprised as was consistent with his serene nature.

Having possessed himself of the lady's hands, he paused and counted ten, during which prudent operation he digested some of the toughest features of the situation.

"It is a most unexpected pleasure," he said, "to salute the late Miss Arabella Greenleaf as 'mother,'" and with an air of the most profound respect he bent forward and kissed the lady on the cheek.

"It's all right, governor," cried Mr. Jack Dorr, turning apologetically to the Colonel, and with an all - comprehensive sweep of his long arms, "I congratulate everybody," and Mr. Jack Dorr thereupon threw himself upon the nearest chair and laughed until the tears came into his eyes.

"Edith opened your cards this morning before I left the house. How's Fred ? Oh, Fred's all right. And Louise ? Louise is a corker, and don't you forget it? Oh, you giddy children ! '' cried Jack after another burst of laughter, '' you are playing the skipper with this story of a son coming on board, and the dear old boy don't tumble.''

'' It is clear there has been no improvement in you, Jack,'' said Mrs. Zaintree (born Greenleaf). '' You are behaving as badly as when you were horrifying all England on the Rotterdam boat.''

When the coincidence of Jack's happening was made plain to the Colonel, and the mystery of the eldest son explained more fully to Jack, it was mutually agreed that the tripartite family relation, offensive and defensive, must be sustained on board the Nautilus.

III

I T was a very pretty family party, the Captain thought, grouped outside the cabin-door, after tea. Jack was so devoted to his very youthful-looking mamma, and the handsome hunting dogs were chasing each other about the deck, and coming back at the call of the Colonel.

Jack was telling Mrs. Zaintree that his real parents, whom he knew she ranked among her most valued friends, were on their way to Duluth, where they would all meet.

"It will be no surprise, this wedding business," said Jack, "for Edith telegraphed them to where they were stopping in Canada as soon as she received your cards."

The Nautilus was at that moment steaming across the beautiful St. Clair, the land a faint blue streak on the horizon. Owing to the extreme heat of the day the sky had been rolling with thunder-caps, and as the sun was setting the gorgeous cloud-forms were sobering down into a dome of infinite delicacy of tints, uniting in almost imperceptible lines, through the purple and golden haze, with the transparent surface of the lake. How enchanting and unreal it was! They seemed to be floating in the centre of a vast globe of color, the sunset below as well as above them. Lying low on the horizon, athwart the delicate purple and lavender clouds, a tattered rope of coal smoke completely surrounded them, now shredded into almost imperceptible strands, and again spread out into eccentric zigzag masses throwing deep shadows on the water.

It was all very soothing and tranquillizing, but Jack grew restive, nevertheless, as the music of dancing on an excursion steamer came floating across the water, and with a genius for spreading the contagion of his own high spirits, he broke the spell of the sunset, and led the way up to a more extended outlook over the bow, where it happened that the Captain was pacing his solitary watch.

It was beautiful to see Jack seat his handsome mamma where the very best view could be had, and then wrap her up to the throat with his own filial hands, against the chill of the evening air.

"I tell you, ma'am," said Captain Webb, "I knew your son was the right sort the minute he come over the rail. I reckon, ma'am, it must be a great comfort to you to have him on board.''

Mrs. Zaintree smiled and said that Jack was always very good to her.

'' It's the way she raised me, skipper,'' said Jack. '' She never laid a hand on me in anger. Taught me love and respect, and that sort o' thing. And the governor here, too, has been quite too indulgent for my good. Makes me too liberal an allowance. Took me to the races before I was out of short clothes and played the winner in my name, and put the stakes in my little bank. Now, I'll leave it to you, Captain, as a fair-minded man,'' and Jack spoke feelingly, '' if the governor has any call to kick, as I am grieved to say he does, when I happen to play the wrong horse ? ''

'' Never mind him, Captain,'' said the Colonel, with some austerity ; '' I have got him now where horses won't trouble him for a few days. What's that double row of peach-trees growing out of the lake just ahead ? It looks like a straight-away course for youngsters, Jack.''

The Captain explained that the curious embankments formed the St. Clair canal, and pointed out the light-houses on either end and the buoys marking the channel of approach. The peach-trees turned out to be brook willows bordering well-worn pathways along either side, and the light-houses looked quite domestic with their vegetable gardens and out-houses. The Colonel inspected the timbered sides, and the steam-dredge moored against the right-hand bank, with the eye of an engineer, and Mrs. Zaintree had the Captain's glass levelled on the club-houses and hotels and cottages that stretched away to the left, beyond the farther light-house, and opposite to the swampy Canadian shore.

When his honored parents grew tired of watching the endless line of lights in cottages, and lanterns hung among green trees, marking pre-empted claims on Government sand-banks, Jack remained to share the Captain's watch and see the Nautilus " tooled " through the river into Lake Huron.

Mr. Jack Dorr made himself doubly agreeable now that he was relieved of parental restraint. By means of some well-chosen and highly flavored stories, which he told with great cleverness, he drew peals of laughter from the two men at the wheel. It afforded a peculiar satisfaction to Jack to stir up these ghostly listeners in the shadowy wheel-house, who

broke the silence at long intervals by a sepul-
chral echo of the Captain's orders.   He was
glad to know that they were awake, and he
would give them something more interesting to
repeat in the forecastle than the gossip of a respectable family.

Jack and the Captain got on bravely.   They
talked local geography and navigation until
Gratiot light hove in sight, and then they talked
dog until the boat was far out in Lake Huron.
The Captain was up on dogs.   In fact he owned
the best bred young Irish setter "in the town
of Ste. Marie or the State of Michigan," and
if things were favorable at the lock they would
have time to run over to his house and look at
it.

"Dog for sale?" asked Jack.   "The deuce
you say.   Strikes me you want big money.
Well, I'll tell you what I'll do, skipper.   If the
governor is as good-natured to-morrow as he
has been to-day, and the pup's points please
me, I'll take it.   Good-night," and Mr. Jack
Dorr went away to his cabin aft.

All the next day the Nautilus labored through
a choppy sea, under a leaden sky; not a
glimpse of land and rarely a ship in sight.   The
anchors had been dropped overboard during
the night, off the entrance to St. Mary's River,

whose tortuous channel was not to be navigated in the dark, but with the first rosy streaks of dawn they were again under way.

When Jack awoke in the early morning the sun was just rising—a great golden ball suspended over the Canada woods. The sun having no particular charm for him just then, he saluted it with some rather uncomplimentary remarks and turned his face to the opposite wall. At the same moment a peculiar shock ran through the timbers of the vessel and he tumbled out and thrust his head into the unwelcome sunlight in time to see the water boiling back from the bow yellow with mud.

"That settles it," said Mr. Jack Dorr, and he turned in again and went to sleep. His repose, however, was short and troubled, for the deck-hands were hammering on iron outside his window. When he dressed himself and came on deck he learned that the rudder-gearing had broken and that the Nautilus was lying helpless across the channel. On the port side a small pine-tree overhung the rail, which, he found on inspection, was attached to the mast of an American tug which had borne down with great promptness on the stranded monster, scenting a job. On the starboard side a Canadian revenue cutter, flying the Union Jack, had already made fast ; and by the number of craft in sight he rightly judged that they would soon be the centre of a considerable fleet.

This interesting prospect rather heightened the relish of Jack's breakfast, which he enjoyed with unusual deliberation, and even lingered behind to worry the parrot. As he lighted his morning cigar and returned to the deck, he was peculiarly in a mood to take the world as it came. It was well that it was so, for the full bloom of Mr. Jack Dorr's serenity was presently disturbed by a familiar voice pronouncing his name, and turning about he confronted his real father, standing in an open gangway alongside a large-eyed Jersey cow.

The meeting was altogether a happy one until the elder Dorr expressed his intention to climb over the boards put up to confine the cow, and come on board the Nautilus.

"Don't do it," said Jack. "I've got one governor on board already ; in fact I am travelling with my parents, and your presence would compromise the family arrangements."

"Hang the family arrangements," cried Jack's father, "I'm coming on board to look into the family arrangements. Do you want to disgrace your mother, you young vagabond ? Do you know she is somewhere on the upper

deck of this steamer overlooking your deviltry
at this moment?"

"Come now, pop; my mother is all right,
Heaven bless her. I am more anxious just now
about the charming lady who sustains that relation to me on board this boat. Easy now,
governor, easy. You know her already."

The elderly gentleman was fast getting beyond the control of his son's peculiar methods
of pacification, and the mild-eyed cow was
staring at him through her halter with a dumb
look of wonderment. It was fortunate for
Jack, at this critical moment, that the Colonel
and his bride emerged from the breakfast
cabin. It was fortunate that Jack saw them
and beckoned them over.

He wisely resigned the task of pacifying his
father into the hands of the charming Mrs.
Zaintree (born Greenleaf), who had already
played the same rôle in his behalf with eminent
success. While the explanations and congratulations were going on between his two governors, Jack relighted his cigar, and turned his attention to the pretty Canadian girls, in sailor
hats, looking over the rail of the passenger
steamer. Sure enough, there was his mother
under an awning, but she didn't see him; and
cautioning the bride to keep out of sight until

he had explained the situation, he clambered through the gangway, leaving his placated father on board the Nautilus.

Jack's mother had it particularly impressed upon her that Arabella Greenleaf was not known to be a bride on board the Nautilus—not by a good many years, Jack said—and then the ladies were allowed to greet each other, at a distance, and throw kisses, and console their warm hearts with the prospect of a completer unburdening in the hotel at Duluth. Jack was so fond of his real mother, and lingered so long in her company, that the passenger steamer came near backing away with him on board. As it was, he slid down a flag-staff and jumped to the deck of the Nautilus, in imminent danger of breaking his bones.

The Canadian boat was well in the offing when Jack walked into his own cabin, and, to his consternation, found his father and the Colonel pledging each other in the Commodore's champagne.

" Well, here is a go," cried Jack. " Mother alone on the other boat, damage repaired, lines cast off, and Heaven help me, with two governors to manage on one ship. Now don't get excited, sir ; it's too late for that sort of thing.

You are here to stay, and she won't miss you until we get up to the locks."

Of course there was a little commotion ; the gentlemen rushed on deck only to find that the two ships were out of hailing distance. Mr. Dorr the elder consoled himself with the belief that his wife would think he was in the barber's shop, or the wheel-house, or the engine-room, or somewhere else on board, for he had a habit of roaming about the steamer. He would get back where he belonged during the passage of the locks of the Saint Mary's, and his wife wouldn't believe him when he related his adventure.

Jack saw the Captain passing, and hailed him. " This gentleman," he said, " is a friend of the governor's ; got left by the passenger steamer. Governor Dorr, Captain Webb. Ex-Governor Dorr of Florida, I believe." It had occurred to Jack's fertile brain that he could thus forestall the danger of a slip of the tongue on his part, and for the remainder of the passage jumble his two governors to his heart's content. " He is rather a distinguished stowaway," continued Jack, " but I reckon we can take care of him up to the locks."

At this he left the governors in the company of the Captain, and hastened away to apprise the

Colonel's bride of the new official dignity he
had conferred on his father. It seemed to Jack
that his old friend Arabella Greenleaf had never
been more charming than he found her at that
moment, in the luxurious cabin of the Nautilus,
flushed with the excitement of the recent meeting and full of enthusiasm in view of the coming
reunion at Duluth.

" And two long days on Lake Superior before we get there," said she, sorrowfully. " I
didn't think yesterday that anything could happen to make this delightful voyage too long.
What a pity it is, when we are all bound to the
same port, we must travel by different ships.
Oh ! Jack," and the lady's face brightened at
the thought, " we must get your mother transferred to the Nautilus while we are passing
through the locks, instead of returning your
father to the Canadian steamer. Come, come,
Jack ; I'll appeal to Captain Webb, as a personal favor."

" Well now, my very enthusiastic friend,"
said Jack, interposing his bulk between the lady
and the door, " you want to compose yourself
first, and bear in mind that the situation is
considerably complicated on this ship already.
The arrangement can undoubtedly be effected.
I suspect that Captain Webb is rather fond of

you—fancy he will grant your request jolly quick. But you must be very cool-headed when you tackle him, and not go blurting out things about my mother, and forgetting that you are a mother yourself.''

'' Oh, dear ! '' sighed the lady, '' what a tangled web we weave——''

'' That's what it is, my dear mamma. But take a little time to consider. There's lots of time. Two good hours. Let's begin,'' and in a moment they were walking up and down the deck outside in consultation.

Close off the port rail a herd of American cows was standing in the edge of the river, affording a soothing object-lesson in patience, as they lazily switched the flies from their sides and dozed ruminant in the broad sunlight. The Canadian passenger steamer was threading the channel in the wake of the Nautilus, its high sides and deck-cabins resembling an Atlantic coaster, and its dingy color suggesting an unpainted farm-house.

IV

A S Jack had predicted, Captain Webb graciously granted Mrs. Zaintree's request,
gallantly intimating that he would turn the ship
into a privateer to oblige her, and the late Arabella Greenleaf made short work of the objec-
tions of the paternal Dorr. By the time they
sighted the granite portal of Lake Superior, the
flashing rapids of the "Soo" tumbling over
the rocks, under the airy trestle of the Canadian
Pacific on the right, and the white houses and
green park of Ste. Marie lying to the left, everything was settled on board the Nautilus. Jack
was to take an extra berth in the Captain's cabin
and resign his own to his parents like a dutiful
son. He fully appreciated the advantages of
the new arrangement, throwing him, as it
would, into extra confidential relations with
the navigator of the Nautilus. It would help
him to maintain his grip on the situation. He
foresaw that the management of two sets of parents, on the same ship, under the critical eyes
of the crew, would require the greatest coolness

on his part. Not that he felt any great anxiety,
or perplexity, or unusual responsibility. Altogether it was the most delightful and inspiring
emergency that Mr. Jack Dorr had ever figured
in. He fairly revelled in it. Instead of perplexing him it nerved him and cooled his
brain.

While the steamers lay below the lock he
found time to go across the park with Captain
Webb and look at his Irish setter, and buy it
too, at a rather exorbitant figure, not because
he wanted it, but because that stroke of liberal-
ity on his part would establish him the more
firmly in the good graces of the Captain.

On their return with the superfluous dog he
found his mother on board. The two ladies
were so absorbed in each other that while the
small fleet of steamers was rising on the boiling
surface of the lock they had shut themselves up
in the cabin. Jack and his two governors, on
the contrary, took a lively interest in the passage through the great granite gateway of the
lakes. Nothing escaped them, from the hy-
draulic working of the lock to the shining soldiers ogling the village girls, and the Chippewa
half-breeds hawking fish freshly taken from the
rapids. They looked regretfully upon the last
barefooted urchin of Ste. Marie watching his

bobber in the sunlight as they steamed away through the open draw of the Canadian Pacific, and passed the light-house onto the bosom of the greatest of the lakes.

Fully determined as Jack was to guard the secret of Mrs. Zaintree, he had no idea of neglecting any favorable opportunity to complicate the situation still further. His serenity always increased as he succeeded in multiplying difficulties, and he proposed to give his genius for comedy full play. He saw a rather humorous possibility at hand, but he was never in a hurry, and after looking thoughtfully down at the green water slipping by, he spent a lazy afternoon reading in the warm sunshine on deck.

In the evening he joined the Captain's watch. The moonlight silvered the smooth surface of the lake ; here and there the lights of a steamer twinkled in the hazy offing ; a huge banner of black smoke trailed back against the canopy of countless stars, and so still was it that the ticking of the wood - work could be heard as the great boat warped along. The listening ears in the shadowy wheel-house were not in the least annoying to Jack ; he found it perfectly convenient to ignore them.

He yawned and broke the silence :

" Rather agreeable elderly people we took

on board to-day?'' (Pause and more silence.) '' Wouldn't spot the old lady for a bride now, would you, skipper?''

'' Go 'way,'' said the Captain, rousing to the occasion.

'' Fact,'' said Jack, '' we met her abroad last year. Old maid then. Second matrimonial trip for the governor. Yes, skipper, they are on their wedding-journey now.''

'' Well,'' said the Captain, after a pause, '' we'll have to make it as pleasant for 'em as we can.''

That very night as Jack lay on his bed, tossing restlessly about in his new and rather narrow quarters, he heard the music of accordions swelling up from the direction of the aftercabins. The Captain was sleeping soundly after his watch, and the see-saw droning of the music was so satisfactory to Jack's mind, and withal so soothing to his spirit, that he fell asleep himself and dreamed that he was leading a serenade.

Anybody could see with half an eye that something had occurred to put new life in the crew of the Nautilus. The stokers sang more lustily at their work. The deck-hands were noisier than ever in the gangway of the forecastle and prolonged their orgies to a later hour.

The Wedding Journey of Mrs. Zaintree

Old Wilhelm's bald head sparkled in the sun like a binnacle that contained a secret. The Captain had a provokingly knowing look in his eye, and the ship itself forged ahead as if it were informed through all its timbers with a new life and energy.

For a plain sailor - man Captain Webb was rather profuse in his attention to the elder lady on board. And this extra devotion did not escape the observation of the younger lady.

To Mrs. Zaintree the crew were plain, civil men, while Mrs. Dorr confessed to her friend that there was an indescribable something in their manner that made her uncomfortable. She might be too sensitive, but she couldn't overcome the feeling. As to that German woman, the cook, her manners were dreadful. When Jack had come into the cabin that morning and kissed her, his own mother (which was very nice of him, it was so very unusual), that creature had sniffed and walked out of the room with the air of a woman insulted. To this Mrs. Zaintree replied by reminding her friend that, so far as Jack was concerned, they had exchanged places for the trip. In the light of this forgotten arrangement Mrs. Dorr could overlook the conduct of the cook, but it was a horrid boat and she should be glad to get

ashore ; and Mrs. Zaintree, too, began to feel that the situation was anything but a pleasant one.
The Captain was conscious that both ladies treated him with a degree of restraint, and held themselves aloof in a rather puzzling way. If there was anything wrong with the ladies, the three gentlemen were doing all they could to make up for it. Three more affable and down-right jolly gentlemen, the Captain was forced to admit, had never gone up on his boat. As to women, in the abstract, he was driven to the conclusion that it was a mistake to have them on board.

When he confided to Jack that there was a screw loose somewhere, and that his navigation among the women was a failure, that young gentleman entered feelingly into the subject of his perplexity, and suggested that the bride might be offended because he had not sufficiently acknowledged her state on board. Some little complimentary demonstration, he thought, might make it all right. As that night's dinner would be the last on board, Jack proposed to make it an extra festive occasion, and volunteered to stand by his friend to the best of his ability. Old Wilhelm was called up and given the necessary directions. Jack spread the news of the dinner among the guests, and when the ladies encountered the Captain on deck they thanked him so graciously that he felt that whatever misunderstanding there might have been, was healed already. Jack was a wonderful manager, and the good feeling on board mounted to enthusiasm. It was a day of days on the great lake. Still water under a cloudless sky. A mirage here and a mirage there, and the ship's glass passing from hand to hand. Steamers in the distance assumed all sorts of fantastic shapes, and bore down on them in the form of curious covered barges, and loomed up with as many as four decks, and shifted themselves into Spanish galleons, and then gradually put off all disguise and steamed by, the very counterparts of the Nautilus.

If Mrs. Zaintree composed herself to read in the shade of the bridge, the show began again in the great azure amphitheatre. Some far-away tow of schooners climbed up into a tower of canvas or turned slow somersaults in the hazy distance and then melted away in the act of turning. Jack said that it was a very creditable little circus to usher in the Captain's dinner, which differed in this respect from dinners on shore, where the mirage commonly unfolded itself afterward.

It was a long time after the green-and-gold parrot cried: "Make way for the Captain," before that promoter of the feast got himself into a sufficiently genial and convivial state of mind to lead off in the speaking. The Captain was so long, in fact, in coming to the point that Jack took the floor in his behalf, and made one of his characteristic after-dinner speeches, in which he said, among other things, that his friend, Captain Webb, of the Nautilus, was well aware of the interesting relations sustained by certain parties on board his ship ; that there were some things which could not be concealed from so shrewd an observer as the Captain ; that his friend the Captain had sought in every way to serve the Commodore's guests, and that, in tendering this little testimonial dinner to the lady who was the distinguished guest of the occasion, he trusted that the others would join him in congratulations and good wishes ; and, finally, he begged to say in behalf of his parents on board, that the courtesy and kindness of the Captain and the marked attention of the crew could never be forgotten by him or by them.

As Jack sat down without having drawn out any of the applause which his ingenious speech merited, the Captain arose promptly and proposed the health of the bride in a few well-chosen remarks, during which he looked hard across the table at Mr. and Mrs. Dorr, who smiled in return and thought it a very clever nautical way of taking them into his confidence at the expense of the Colonel, and not so trying to the bride as if he had stared directly at her.

Of course the Colonel felt called upon to respond, which he did, after a brief hesitation, by proposing the health of Captain Webb of the Nautilus, which sentiment Mr. and Mrs. Dorr applauded so heartily that the Captain was fain to be satisfied with their response by proxy, although he was a good deal surprised that an ex-Governor should not be a fluent after-dinner speaker.

The Captain was mightily pleased with the success of his little banquet, and his guests were so surprisingly jolly over it that he felt himself quite a social lion. They were so very merry that they would never desert him until they got the first glimpse of the far-away lights of Duluth. Jack and his two governors, with their cigars, and the ladies in warm wraps, kept the deck far into the night, and made it very lively for the men at the wheel. The long lines of electric lights on the granite hill-

side flashed row above row, and shot long
lances into the lake, and the great shadowy
elevators were piled up against the western sky
before ever the Captain was left alone to ponder
on the wonderful cleverness of Jack's management, and rub his hands in gleeful memory of
his own shrewdness and penetration.

"A bridal party go up on my boat and I
not know it at sight!" thought the Captain.
"Not much — not if they were turned of
ninety."

"You are a sly one, Governor Dorr," he
muttered to himself as he was parting with his
guests on the wharf next morning. "Mighty
sly, Governor, but you must get the rice out
of your hair before you come on board the
Nautilus."

And to Mrs. Zaintree, he said :

"You are a pattern mother of a pattern son,
ma'am, and if I did think you a bit unfeeling
when Jack was coming on board it's because
I'm not a society man, ma'am, and didn't
know the thoroughbred trick."

Uncle Obadiah's Uncle Billy

UNCLE OBADIAH'S UNCLE BILLY

THE spare figure of the old man on the houseless country road, pushing on into the twilight with a weary, swinging tread, was as erect under its weight of fourscore years as that of any boy of fifty. The spare figure melted into the leafless woods, and reappeared a little later on the hill, very tall and very mysterious against the fading light. A knapsack as thin and shrunken as the muscles of the old man clung close to his square shoulders, and the bronze star, made of the metal of captured cannon, rattled against a medal for personal service, and the music cheered his old heart.

Although it was not yet the first of March, the rank smell of the mellow earth proclaimed the absence of frost, and the brook at the roadside ran swollen and yellow between its banks. The old man in blue asked the way to the village of a boy who was trotting in the gravel behind the crackling hoofs of a white cow, and then added in a weary voice:

" Perhaps you might know. my lad, of a

youngster hereabouts of the name of Frederick
Brown ? ''

But the boy only stared, and then ran away,
as if he had seen a ghost. He did not know
Private Obadiah Brown, of six wounds and one
medal : one wound received in storming the
outworks of Atlanta ; four, in the heart, for the
sons he had buried on as many bloody fields ;
and the sixth for his youngest boy, '' missing ''
after the battle. And this was the wound that
had never healed, and this was the boy he had
never given up. All the years that had passed
since his discharge, with unfaltering courage
and undying hope he had kept up the weary
search, growing old and childish, with a youth
of twenty in his vision, who should have been
a man of fifty — so completely had the two
changed places. He had passed the short win-
ters at many soldiers' homes in many States,
ready to start afresh in the spring on roads
that led through new towns and cities, armed
with the bronze star and the countersign and
the fraternal grip, potent to open the doors and
the hearts of the Grand Army posts.

Although in his restless journeying he was always coming to some new town or lodging-
place, it better fits his character of wanderer
that he was always leaving friends and firesides

—the known behind and the unknown fleeing before him—always going, going.

While the form of the boy faded into the bosky landscape, the cow grew whiter with the growing darkness, and preceded the old man like a cloud by night, until he came in sight of the village belfry sprinkled around with early stars. It was too dark to see the face of the clock, but as he approached the hammer beat three strokes, and then was still.

This was encouraging.

The tavern was a little further on, and Private Obadiah Brown turned in at the open door. The landlord was behind the dismantled bar, trimming the oil-lamps. The quick eye of the old man caught the light on a small bronze button in the lapel of the landlord's coat, and the landlord took in the star and medal on the other's breast, and the two men were friends in an instant, and, no customers being present to interfere, were promptly off on their old campaigns, with chuckles, and hand-shakes, and "you bets," and "Grant fit it out on them lines, shure," and "They couldn't fool Uncle Billy."

The tavern-keeper forgot to offer the fly-blown register, which had not secured an autograph in a week, with the spluttering pen out of the tumbler of bird-shot, and the old man forgot his knapsack and his hunger and his rheumatics, until the more important functions of comradeship had been duly performed to their common satisfaction.

Private Obadiah Brown felt refreshed when supper was done. Indeed, he had not been overtired on his arrival, late as the hour was, for he had walked only a few miles since he had mended his last clock.

About the soft-coal fire, which flickered and blazed in the open grate before the bar, a few of the old soldiers thereabouts, with metal buttons on their vests, had chanced in for an evening's lounge, and were ready to give a fraternal greeting to Uncle Obadiah when that ancient veteran should reappear.

The blacksmith, who had been a sergeant in a light battery, by a sort of acknowledged village supremacy was the first to present himself.

" I reckon, comrade," he said, as he put out his great hairy arm, and the two exchanged the regulation grip, " as how you must outrank us all, countin' by years."

" I'm turned of eighty," said Uncle Obadiah, straightening himself with soldierly pride, and looking across at the old boys, each standing unconsciously at "attention" in front of his arm-chair. " Old enough to be a major-giner-al, an' not too old nur too proud to be a high private."

"This here old vet," continued the sergeant-blacksmith, giving a hearty whack to the first old farmer's back, "is Comrade Stover of the 81st Infantry, an' he'll give ye all the hand he's got, an' he can drive a pair o' young hosses as well as the next one; an' him with the bow legs," giving Uncle Obadiah a sly poke in the ribs, "is Comrade Hitch of the Fourteenth Cavalry (never run no great resk o' bein' hurt). An' this next one, on crutches, is Comrade Cist from Georgy, as fit on the other side, an' left his leg on Missionary Ridge."

"I'm truly sorry 'bout the leg, comrade." cried Uncle Obadiah, marching over to give an extra-energetic shake to the last man's hand, "an' I've no doubt you did yer duty as you saw it. But, comrades, I had a boy, an' he was the last o' five, jest risen twenty, who went into that fight on Missionary, as bright and chipper as a lark, an' ef he'd 'a' left a leg there I'd 'a' had somethin' to remember him by ; but instead he jest disappeared out o' hand, comrades, an' it's him I'm lookin' for. Jest risen twenty—favors me when I was that old— light-complected, with blue eyes — powerful

chipper, and answers to the name o' Frederick
Brown. Have airy one o' you comrades seen
or heard of sich a boy goin' by the name o'
Frederick Brown?''

The comrades maintained a respectful silence,
and the eager look of inquiry which had overspread the old man's face faded into an expression of weariness, and with a deep-drawn
sigh he sank into a chair.

"It's all right, comrades: I didn't much
think you knew my boy, but if I could once
meet up with Uncle Billy, he'd tell me all
about him. Uncle Billy knew him well. He
hilt his horse one day. No one once seein'
my boy could easy forgit him, an' Uncle Billy
never forgot a human being as did him a favor.
They say he was terrible crusty sometimes, and
them under-ginerals was mortal afeared of him
when he was riled, but he always had a smile
an' a kind word for the boys. I might 'a'
writ him a letter about Frederick, but writin'
wouldn't be like talkin' to Uncle Billy face to
face; an', you see, I wanted to see him once
more afore I died, an' appeal to him like a
father to a father, an' show him that I kep' the
old medal faithful.'' Uncle Obadiah lifted the
bronze coin from his breast and gazed fondly
on his treasure.

" Uncle Billy didn't just give it to me with his own hands, comrades, but he had a letter writ to the whole army givin' it from him to me. I was young then, comrades—only fifty-two—an' when the gineral's aide pinned it on my blouse front before the colonel an' the whole regiment—parade rest—he gave me another letter, an' ev'ry word of it was writ by Uncle Billy with his own name signed to it : 'William Tecumseh Sherman, Major-Gineral Commanding, to Private Obadiah Brown.' An' I hain't never parted with that letter, comrades, not for a day.''

With trembling fingers Uncle Obadiah unbuttoned his tightly fitting, threadbare, military-looking coat, and drew from the breast pocket a formidable package, from which he undid wrapper after wrapper until he came to an official paper, yellow with age. Then he got up and shuffled over to the bar, with all the comrades crowding eagerly about him ; and after the boards had been wiped clear of dust and moisture, he spread the precious paper out on its tattered wrappers.

" Uncle Billy didn't write a copy hand, boys,'' said the old man, gloating over the eager study of the veterans as they spelled out the words. " My Frederick could 'a' give'

him lessons; but there 'tis, comrades, an'
there's his whole name put to it. If he didn't
write a copy hand, he could command an army,
Uncle Billy could.''

The landlord, the blacksmith, Comrade Stover, and Comrade Hitch of the cavalry, every-
one a veteran of the Army of the Tennessee,
and Comrade Cist from Georgia, leaning on his
crutches, regarded the yellow paper with as much
reverence as if it had been a newly discovered
chapter of the sacred Scriptures, and in their
eyes Uncle Obadiah was as big a man as a
prophet.

Each old soldier who wore the bronze button
had something to tell to the praise and glory
of his old commander and personal Uncle Billy,
and Private Obadiah Brown told them how in
'86 he had tramped all the way to St. Louis to
see the general and find out the secret of his
boy's whereabouts, and how his idol had just
sold his Western home and gone to live in a
far-off Eastern city; how he had been hoarding
his money ever since, what he could save from
his earnings and his pension, and how the sum
was nearly large enough for the stupendous un-
dertaking of a journey by rail to New York,
where he very soon expected to see his Uncle
Billy face to face, and to put an end to the

mystery ; for he had no doubt of the absolute omniscience of his old commander.

"Well, now, Comrade Brown," said Comrade Stover, knocking the ash out of his pipe on the heel of his cowhide boot, "when you git to see old Uncle Billy, you can tell him that when you was out here in Ohio you met up with one of the marchin' Eighty-first, an' that his legs was good as new."

"There was a man here a couple o' year back," said the landlord, leaning over the bar until his face was inscrutable in the shadow, "what had been on to New York, an' he told me that he seen old Uncle Billy a-settin' in a gold box to the theatre with his regimentals on, an' his yaller belt, an' that folks looked at the gold box more'n they did at the play. An' how, by an' by, the West Point cadets, settin' down below, jumped up an' hurrahed for Gineral Sherman, till the play had to stop whilst Uncle Billy made a speech. He said the gineral talked to them kids as plain as any old farmer, givin' 'em good advice, his little beads o' eyes twinklin' in his head, an' his hook-nose rangin' over his stubby white mustache an' beard, like a ten-pounder Parrot squintin' over slashed timber."

"Hooray!" piped Uncle Obadiah, bright-

ening up ; " they couldn't flank Uncle Billy ef
they had him shet up in a nest o' gold boxes."

" 'That's a fact," said the landlord ; "ef old
Uncle Billy hadn't ordered them cadets to
keep quiet, the theatre wouldn't 'a' been let
out yet."

It was pleasant to see how kindly the old
soldiers took to Uncle Obadiah, and how well
they agreed with one another, and, in short,
what very mild old fellows they were, notwithstanding their youthful exploits.

" It's gittin' ruther late," observed the tavern - keeper at last, turning down one of the
dingy oil - lamps to emphasize his meaning.
" Comrade Brown ain't leavin' us jest yet,
havin' a considerable engagement 'long o' the
town clock. When he gits that strikin' right
ag'in, Hitch an' Cist 'll have to go to bed at
nine, or have a fallin' out with the meetin'
folks."

So the old comrades quietly filed out into
the night, leaving Private Obadiah Brown to
get some needed rest before he undertook the
job of mending in the belfry. While he was
waiting for his host to show him the way to
bed, he fell to listening, in a half-conscious
way, to the frying of the fat coal in the grate.
and to the sound of the rising wind outside as

it rattled the wooden shutters against the windows. His chin was settling on his breast for
weariness when the stumping sound of a crutch
on the platform outside brought him back to
himself, and the door was gently pushed open
to admit the head of Comrade Cist from Georgia, who said that if he should not see him in
the morning he reckoned he wouldn't forget to
show the general that letter.

When Private Obadiah Brown awoke, the
sun was shining brightly, and the crazy old
town clock was striking two. It had just got
on to three bells, an hour later, when Comrade
Stover drove by with a wagon-load of wood.

"It's a-callin' to ye," cried Comrade Stover, gayly saluting with the stump of his right
forearm. "'Pears like it's ruther short o'
breath, Comrade Brown. Putty nigh time ye
was gittin' yer invalid hospital set up in the
belfry, an' runnin' out the yaller flag — he!
he! The ball's open."

The sun was unusually warm for a morning
in February, and the ice that had beaten in, in
the form of sleet, and had crusted the wooden
shield above the works of the old clock, was
melting drop by drop and spattering on the
belfry floor, where Uncle Obadiah had opened
his thin knapsack and spread out his small

store of professional tools and cords and wheels. The air as it came in through the blistered green blinds had no power to chill the thinnest blood in the oldest veins. Uncle Obadiah had climbed upon a short ladder, and beaten down a last year's swallow's nest or two, before he put on his "spec's" to take a critical look at the works and to plan his campaign. The ropes which held the weights were certainly badly worn, and must be replaced with new ones. It taxed the old man's strength to lift the heavy iron and detach it from the rusty hook. He had just accomplished the separation, and held the weight poised over the opening in the floor cut away for its natural descent between the old beams and braces, when the urchin who had refused to direct him to the village came clambering up the stairs, all out of breath.

" I say, granddad—now — General Sherman's dead."

Down fell the iron weight, splintering the wood and crashing through the plastering, and making the old stairs rock and shiver as if the belfry itself were tumbling. Uncle Obadiah backed down until his feet rested on the firm boards, and glared through his glasses at the frightened boy.

" You ought to be whipped, you rascal! I'm eighty year——"

" It's true," said the boy. " Si Wilkins, the tavern-keeper, told me to come an' tell ye."

Uncle Obadiah tottered over to the wall, and looked down through the blinds, muttering in his incredulity as he went. There stood Comrade Stover's team alone in the road. A woman at a house door was shading her eyes with her hand and looking out, much as he was. The blacksmith, bareheaded, was running up the path from his shop with a red-hot horseshoe in his pincers.

Uncle Obadiah began to fear the truth, and to feel his way down the rickety belfry stairs.

" No, no! " he muttered to himself; " he was young, an' I'm risin' eighty. Perhaps ye might 'a' heard of a youngster by the name of Frederick Brown. No, no! It ain't true."

The clock-weight had burst its way through lath and wooden ceilings, and as the old man tottered out upon the sunlit porch, it lay in his path on the shattered planks.

The railway ran through the valley, a mile from the village, but there was no telegraph-operator at the small station. The news had come over from a neighboring town, and come so tardily that there was a rumor of the great military funeral in New York, which should, that very morning, be passing down the long avenue, between the ranks of the uncovered multitude, amidst the tolling of bells and the beating of muffled drums, a flowing stream of funeral dirges. In truth, at the very moment when the clock-weight fell from the hand of Uncle Obadiah, eight sergeants were raising all that remained of his Uncle Billy, draped in the folds of the flag he had loved, to its place aloft on the caisson catafalque. The artillery drivers were in their saddles ready at the word to draw the caisson down the long avenue, as a soldier should take his last ride. The black charger stood behind, and all the city streets for miles were massed with posts of grizzled veterans, and the serried ranks of national troops and sailors from the fleet, and the brilliant regiments of citizen soldiery, and the historic corps of cadets, come to honor the last American general, whom they had long regarded as their military father—the same Uncle Billy whom they had cheered until they were hoarse, in his gold box.

When Uncle Obadiah shuffled out upon the sunlit porch, past the fallen clock-weight, all this was going on five hundred miles away, in the presence of the President of the Republic, the judges of the Supreme Court, the senators and generals and representatives of the people, and Uncle Obadiah was as unaware of it all as was Uncle Billy himself.

The blacksmith shut up his shop. Comrade Stover drove his empty wagon home, and returned to the village. Comrade Hitch of the cavalry left his plough in the furrow, and came up to the general rendezvous with his bronze star pinned to his coat. Si Wilkins furbished up his metal button, and bought some yards of black cloth, with a surprising recklessness of cost, to drape the front of his tavern. Comrade Cist from Georgia covered up his leather-seated bench, and hobbled over to the tavern, to find Uncle Obadiah crooning over the fire, with trembling lips and a dazed look in his watery eyes.

"I can't ever show him the letter," muttered Uncle Obadiah when he saw the other, "nor yet the medal, give' from him to me, I've kep' so long. Have any of you comrades heard of a youngster that answers to the name o' Frederick Brown?"

There was no more work for the old comrades that day, and when, later, news came that the funeral train bearing the remains of their old general was already speeding on its way from the banks of the Hudson to the shores of the Mississippi, flying through the great cities and the smallest villages, and never halting except to exchange one powerful engine for another, and that the way of the swift pageant lay over the line in the valley, they knew that Sherman Post—their post—would come marching over from the county town with all the comrades, and the old flags, and the fifes and drums, and they began making preparations to receive them.

With furled flags and more black cloth they draped the little railway station, and helped Comrade Si Wilkins to provision his tavern for a larger crowd than it had held for many a day.

It was a long line of graybeards that flanked the supper-table, and the lamplight danced on stars and medals and badges and no end of brass buttons. Private Obadiah Brown sat at the head of the board, and, by way of grace, asked if any one of the comrades present had heard of "a youngster answerin' to the name o' Frederick Brown," and ate but little, and had his knapsack fetched from the belfry floor, because he said he should not feel dressed without it.

The funeral train was full three hundred miles away, and it was early bedtime, despite the silence of the village clock, when ranks were formed in front of the tavern door. Comrade Cist from Georgia, who couldn't hope to keep up with the march, and didn't feel sure that he belonged in the column, together with Uncle Obadiah, whose impatience outran that of all the others, had already started on before. The post's new banner was furled and draped in black, but the tattered old battle-flags, in all their homely nakedness, fluttered free beneath their old eagles, showing along the frayed-out stripes at least half the letters of each of the famous battles of the Army of the Tennessee. Away ahead in the darkness Comrade Cist and Uncle Obadiah heard the regular thump, thump of the bass drum, and held up their heads and quickened their pace with the old instinct born of martial habit.

" Jest to think," said Uncle Obadiah, feeling his shuffling way in the darkness, " Uncle Billy is comin' tearin' like them snortin' engines used to come into a captured town, loaded down with commissaries."

" Jest to think," mused Comrade Cist from Georgia, stumping on his crutches.

" An he was a young man," continued Un-

cle Obadiah, "an' I'm turned of eighty, an'
keepin' good time yet; an' him—did I say
eighty?—tutt—I'm only fifty, an' Uncle Billy
a matter o' forty. Harkee, prisoner, you'll see
a sight when Uncle Billy comes, ridin' in front
of his ginerals—mighty stiff and plain himself,
but miles o' horses an' acres o' gold lace an'
plumes behind him. Did they say you fit on
t'other side? An' ruther badly hurt, I guess
—never you worry, boy; I'll make it right
with Uncle Billy. I'll tell him how you did
yer duty as you saw it, an' he'll send you back
to hospital."

"I'm much obleeged," said Comrade Cist
from Georgia.

"Halt! Rest!" commanded Uncle Obadiah. "It's black as cats. What regiment is
that a-marchin' by? It does me good to hear
the belts an' canteens rattle. They're his soldiers, prisoner, but they'll treat you like a
prince, because you're hurt. I wonder if any
o' them comrades have heard of a youngster
that answers to the name o' Frederick Brown.
What matter? Uncle Billy is comin' to tell me
all about it—an' I'm eighty—fifty—how old
am I, comrade?"

"I reckon you're turned of eighty," said
Comrade Cist from Georgia.

" It may be," said Uncle Obadiah.

Before the post drew up at the station, a cold, drizzling rain had set in, and the little waiting-room was already filled. The way-trains had passed from east and west, bearing news of what was going on along the line. To the east, the general's old veterans were massing in city and village, in the night and in the storm, baring their heads and dipping their ragged flags to the flying special as it flashed through the darkness; and to the west, when the day should dawn, the school-children, with songs and winter flowers, would reinforce the Grand Army.

The old soldiers built ruddy fires alongside the track, laying ruthless hands on broken fence-rails and discarded railroad ties, and constructed shelters from the rain as promptly as they had ever thrown up ten miles of log and earth breastworks under Uncle Billy's orders; and Private Obadiah Brown—six wounds and one medal—and Comrade Cist from Georgia—two crutches and one leg—were snugly housed in the warmest corner by the first fire.

And so while the silent sergeants were standing guard in the draped funeral car, heavy with the odor of flowers, and the rivers and towns were flowing east under the wheels of the gliding train, the simple veterans, around the smoky fires hissing with raindrops, were singing the old songs, as they waited with throbbing hearts : " Tramp, tramp, tramp, the boys are marching," " John Brown's body lies a-moldering in the ground," and " We are tenting tonight on the old camp-ground."

As the long night wore on, each one had some story to tell of the old days ; and it was Uncle Billy here and Uncle Billy there— Uncle Billy in his shirt-sleeves on the porch of his log hut, and Uncle Billy at the head of his brilliant staff, surrounded by his generals, and all the roads full of cavalry, and all the air full of music.

Once Uncle Obadiah fell asleep, and awoke with a start, and with the old question on his lips, to find the blacksmith replenishing the fire, and Comrade Stover punctuating his story with the stump of his right arm, and Comrade Cist from Georgia snoring lustily at his side.

"Somethin' might 'a' happened to the road," said Uncle Obadiah ; " but he was drefful quick at buildin' bridges an' layin' gaps o' track. Uncle Billy ain't a-travellin' to-night without a construction train ahead." And then, laying his hand on the blacksmith's arm, " Don't let me forgit to show him the medal an' the letter writ from him to me. You're strong an' young, an' you must make me a way through the ginerals. I must have a word with him, comrade, face to face. I've been a-waitin' thirty year——''

'' Uncle Obadiah ain't jest awake yit,'' observed Comrade Stover.

'' He's gone clean daft, has Comrade Brown,'' said the blacksmith, dropping the heavy stick he held over the hissing fire, and standing stiff and black against the leaping flames. And then, in a louder tone: '' This here is a bad storm, Comrade Brown; have ye made out to keep dry and warm?''

'' I've seen worse,'' said Uncle Obadiah. '' I've seen worse. There was Kenesaw an' the storm o' Vicksburg. What are we lyin' here for?'' cried the old man, starting to his feet. '' We'll have our orders quick enough when Uncle Billy gits here. Have you heard the batteries yet, boys?''

'' Never mind the batteries,'' said the blacksmith, putting out his strong arm to restrain Private Obadiah Brown, who would have gone out into the rain. '' The colonel's got his orders. We're to lay right here till Uncle Billy comes. Didn't you see the orderly ride by?''

"Yes, I did," said Uncle Obadiah; "I heard his sabre jingle, an' the spatter of the water as his horse trotted past. I thought I saw the yellow envelope stuffed underneath his belt."

"So you did," said the blacksmith, as he and Comrade Stover gently forced the old man back to his seat. "We're to stay right here till Uncle Billy comes. Them's his orders."

"His orders," muttered Uncle Obadiah, calming down with that assurance. "He won't be far behind his orders. I'll lay down alongside my prisoner, here, till the doctors come. They can't flank Uncle Billy."

So the old man fell asleep with a childish trust in his great commander; and that he might get the rest his old bones needed, his comrades talked in lower tones around the fire. Uncle Obadiah was not the only veteran asleep beside the fires, for the vigil had been a long one, and although the rain was falling steadily, there was just a perceptible graying of the darkness which betokened the near approach of day.

HARK! Miles to the east, where the next town lies, they hear the prolonged scream of a locomotive. Promptly the drum beats, but not so fast as the thumping hearts of the old soldiers.

" That's Uncle Billy coming," breaks from every lip, and then every lip is still.

To the bugle blowing the " assembly," the veterans fall silently in line, dressed on the old flags at the centre, the fires burning brightly behind them, and the rain falling steadily upon them. Each man is thinking his own thoughts. In the distance they hear the rolling of the train, but the sound is scarcely louder than the hissing of the raindrops on the fires, or the tinkling of the bronze stars against the medals.

Now it has turned the wall of the intervening mountain. The great engine pants in furious crescendo. The swelling roar of the monster is like the coming of a great shell. The dazzling headlight glares through the trees. The iron rails, wet and slippery, turn to parallels of glittering gold. As if it were the passing spirit of their great commander, the fierce light flashes along the ranks of his old veterans, gleaming for an instant on bared heads and tearful faces, and gilding once more the fragmentary names of his battles on their ragged standards, and then leaves the old line in redoubled darkness.

And, through it all, there are two beside the fires whom the bugles and the drum-beats fail to awaken. Of the two only one can be aroused, and that one Comrade Cist from Georgia.

The Missing Evidence in
"The People *vs.* Dangerking"

THE MISSING EVIDENCE IN "THE PEOPLE *VS*. DANGERKING"

I

IN the spring of 1891, after having spent the month of February in a run through southern Italy with my photographic outfit, I had returned to Rome with ten days at my disposal before my train left for Naples, where I had taken my return passage for New York. I had arrived in the night, and after sleeping until a rather late hour in the morning, had breakfasted in my room, so that it must have been something after ten o'clock when, camera in hand, I descended to the lobby of the hotel. After glancing at the register I seated myself before an open window and looked out on the modern Roman Concourse, with the comfortable indifference of an experienced traveller, whose itinerary is irrevocably fixed to his entire satisfaction. If I felt any personal anxiety it was in no degree disquieting, and related only to the artistic quality of the exposures I had

made, and to the possibilities of the develop-
ments with which I proposed to electrify my
fellow-amateurs of the Club on my return.

I was lazily considering where I should go
for the day, in search of picturesque effects of
light and shade nestling in environments suited
to my taste, with entire indifference to, nay,
even with a sort of professional contempt for,
the historic monuments of the Eternal City,
preferring a sleepy donkey in transparent half-
lights, to the architectural glories of St. Peter's,
when I realized that a figure had crossed the
marble pavement and was standing at my side.

"I beg your pardon," said the stranger, in
a pleasant voice ; "you are Dr. Lattimer, of
the Amateur Photographers' Society of New
York. I am Philip Coe, of St. Louis. I saw
your Japanese work last winter at the Club's
exhibition, and I am very glad to meet you."

Whereupon Mr. Philip Coe and I shook
hands, exchanged cards, and sat down to an
animated discussion of developers and solutions
and improved lenses, as if we had been known
to each other for years instead of for minutes.
My new-found enthusiast was rather a handsome man, of rising thirty, a decided blond,
of an easy and affable manner, unimpeachable
costume. and having a clear gray eye which be-

tokens that order of quick intelligence which forms conclusions intuitively and acts promptly —in short, a man who, to use an Americanism, rarely " gets left " in his combinations.

I am a particular admirer of that sort of man. I pride myself on keeping my faculties well in hand, such as they are, and acting in an emergency without any unnecessary delay. This similarity of temperament, then, together with similarity of pursuits, in our vacation time, commended Mr. Philip Coe, of St. Louis, to my esteem and approval, and his pleasant, unobtrusive ways lent themselves to the daily improvement of our agreeable relations during that week which we spent together in Rome. His collection of work was a very creditable one, and in the professional excursions we took together I was greatly impressed with the cleverness he evinced in seizing the happy instant in a moving composition, and the entire absence of that unfortunate hesitancy which too often renders the most experienced amateur a thought too late in his exposure. My companion was always perfectly cool, with plenty of nerve and no perceptible nerves, and I admired him for that distinguishing peculiarity.

He confided to me that he had been interested in photography but little more than a

year. Having concluded a remarkably success·
ful operation in stocks, he had retired from
active business, and come abroad for the undisturbed enjoyment of his new fad, in which
he was ambitious to distinguish himself; and
when he returned to America, he should rely
on my friendly offices to make him a member
of the New York Society.

I had arranged to return to Naples to take
my steamer, and to go down leisurely by rail
the day before she sailed.

Philip Coe had set no definite time for his
return to America, but would be off in a few
days for a flying visit to Algeria, and then it
was his purpose to push up into Polish Russia
for part of the summer. At all events, with
his admirable photographic outfit and his professional enthusiasm, I expected great things of
his summer's work, which he would bring home
before the winter meetings of the Society. He
was altogether such a cool customer, so full of
resource and tact and cleverness, that I had no
fear for him on the burning sands of Africa or
among the petty civil officers of the Czar, and
I only ventured to advise him to avoid the
neighborhood of military works as he would
shun the plague.

On the evening before we separated, as we

were lingering together over a last bottle of Asti Spumanti in the Trattorea Fiorelli, which had come to be a favorite resort in our wanderings about Rome, my companion said : " By the way, Doctor, one never knows what those Muscovite officials may do in the way of seizing on a man's valuables. I have a paper in my pocket which I would be obliged to you if you would take charge of until I see you in New York." He searched the paper out from among others in his pocket-book and passed it over to me. La padrona brought an envelope in which I sealed up the paper, and Philip Coe wrote his name and the date across the end of the package, and soon after we turned out of No. 4 Via Colonnetti and made our way in the moonlight across the Corso and through the quaint streets leading to our hotel.

On the following day but one, I boarded the Utopia at Naples *en route* for New York. The prospective passage was not wildly entrancing, with only seventeen cabin passengers on board and more than eight hundred emigrants in the steerage.

We had fair weather and an uneventful passage until the afternoon of Tuesday, March 17th, when the ship began to labor heavily against head - winds and high seas. Despite

the rain which was driving in our teeth, I
kept the deck until the great mass of Gibraltar
loomed vaguely through the thick atmosphere
off our starboard bow, and then, learning that
the Captain had decided to stand into the
harbor and lie by until morning, I retired to
my cabin. It was now growing dark, but the
lights were burning in the gangways and all
was quiet below decks. I hoped the sky would
clear by morning, so that I could try my
camera on the famous fortress as well as on
some of the English ironclads at anchor in the
harbor.

The bullseyes were closed, and the spume
and spray were so thick outside that nothing
could be seen beyond the streaming glass, and
although the ship trembled from stem to stern
as she labored against wind and current, I had
such implicit confidence in the skill of her officers and crew that I stretched myself on my
berth with something of the comfortable feeling
of a man before a glowing fire listening to the
rain beating on the roof and to the wind howl-
ing in the chimney. My eye fell on the particular leather bag in which I had packed my
precious, undeveloped negatives, standing on
the floor over against the side of the ship, and
lulled by the music of the storm, my imagina-

tion was revelling in the gradual development
of the latent images imprisoned on the surfaces
of those magical dry plates. The atmosphere
of my state-room was more than comfortably
warm, and I had removed my shoes and outer
clothing the more perfectly to yield myself to
the luxury of my surroundings. The laboring
of the ship was indicated by such regularity of
beating against head-seas, and such a soothing
monotony of shivering throes that, when a
thud broke the uniformity of sound followed
by an entire change of motion and scurrying
of feet on the deck above, I sprang out of my
berth thoroughly alarmed, opened my door,
and stepped into the gangway. I had caught
up a heavy storm ulster, and turning this about
me as I ascended to the deck, regardless of my
stockinged feet, I looked out into the pelting
rain. The blanched face of one of the officers
as he hurried past me into the spume, which
rendered objects at a few paces invisible, con-
firmed my worst fears, and going quickly to
the side of the ship, which was for the moment
ominously steady, I looked over the rail. By
instinct or by accident, I had arrived directly
over the point of contact where the invisible
monster had pierced the side of the Utopia,
and indistinct as my vision was, I could see a

vast dark cavity in the hull into which the whole broadside of the sea was pouring like a maelstrom. It may have been three minutes after the first shock of the collision, and while I moved forward by an instinct of repulsion from the inflowing torrent, when I thought I felt a perceptible settling of the ship. In the direction of what I believed to be the shore, a wet light made a soft yellowish spot in the blanket of spray. I remember with awful distinctness the sounds that greeted my ears, in which the throb of the engines had no part, and the thoughts that flashed through my brain while my eyes were fixed on the warmth of that vague light. A babel of terrified voices rose from between decks, dulled in volume by the wind and rain. There was a sharp rattle like the passing of wheels, for which I can suggest no explanation, and suddenly I seemed to see the clear gray eyes of Philip Coe fixed on mine.

There was another movement of the deck under my feet, I swung myself to the starboard rail by the foremast shrouds, and plunged outward into the sea.

I remember the cold, strangling shock as my body struck the water, the prickling sensation in my nose, the utter blackness instead of the

usual cool green color of the sea as I looked
about me with wide-open eyes, while for an instant I stood upright, poised in its depth, and
then the buoyant sensation of rising to the surface, which I hastened by a familiar movement
of the hands. As my head popped above the
water a blinding sheet of spray struck me in
the face like a whip-lash. Remembering that
the ship had been steaming against a head-wind,
blowing from nearly due east, I laid my course
to the right across that of the wind, and turning my face away from the blowing spray, I
swam with an easy stroke in what I believed to
be the direction of the shore. It was a scudding rather than a high sea, and with the back
of my head laid over against the gusts of salt
spume, I could breathe easily and had perfect
confidence in my ability to sustain myself for a
half-hour, if I could hold out so long against
the chilling influence of the March sea. I was
so little disturbed in mind, that I distinctly
remember the grotesque thought coming to me
for the first time, that the day was the famous
anniversary of St. Patrick. I thought I heard
the splash of someone swimming behind me,
but it was now so dark that I could scarcely see
my length into the scud and gloom. I called
twice, but got no answer. I had either been

mistaken or the other unfortunate had yielded to the waves, and gone down to a watery grave at the bottom of that treacherous sea. The thought was anything but reassuring, and as I already began to feel the benumbing effect of the cold, I inflated my lungs to their utmost and kicked my feet together to keep up circulation.

Suddenly a strong light shot over the water from my right, defining a broad bar across the mist, and by the time I had turned to swim in that direction, a still brighter light shot out from the very course I had abandoned. I knew that these were search-lights from the English iron-clads at anchor in the roadstead. The friendly bars of light shifted about and increased in number, and desperate as my situation was, brought to mind the bars of electric light lying out from the tower of Madison Square Garden on election night. Under their combined influence the surface of the sea took on a ghostly illumination, enabling me to look about me for some distance, although I could discern nothing in the direction whence the lights came. Just then I again heard the puffing of the swimmer behind me. I looked over my shoulder. A horribly black head protruded above the water, set with two gleaming eyes which suggested some sea-monster rather than a fellow-man. In another moment I recognized it as the head of a dog, and when presently it came alongside as if craving human help, or at least human companionship, I found myself in the company of a huge Newfoundland. His great brown eyes were full of appealing light, and turned on me as if he would have licked my face. I threw my arm over his neck, and called him "old chap," and I am sure we both felt better after that exchange of civilities. Stupid fellow that he was, he seemed to think that a little of my weight thrown across his shaggy shoulders insured his safety, and I felt that while I accepted his help for the time being, an opportunity would soon come when my good offices would be a sufficient return therefor. It was no longer a question of swimming only, but of endurance against the benumbing sea. I felt that I was growing weak. I knew my companion would endure the cold longer than I could. A strong current was drifting us along under the brightest bar of light. I thought I saw something of the hull and spars of a great ship close in front of us. I cried aloud for help. I hooked my arm more tightly about the neck of the dog. I thought I saw a movement close upon us and then I lost consciousness, overcome

by the cold and exertion. I felt no sense of
giving up or yielding to despair, but rather
that I was falling into the arms of some mysterious power to which I shifted all responsibility,
so that, when I returned to consciousness, I was
not in the least surprised to find myself snugly
tucked away in a bunk of H. M. S. Camperdown. My first inquiry was for the fate of my
swimming mate, who spoke for himself, project-
ing his great paws on the bed and making va-
rious dumb signs of joy at my awakening. The
delightful sense of warmth enveloping body and
brain seemed to represent the sum of all earthly
bliss, and I straightway fell off into a deep sleep
which lasted for twelve hours, so that, when I
awoke again it was late in the day following
the disaster, and the small proportion of the
rescued to the number of souls on board the ill-
fated ship, was already cared for.

A rather nondescript suit of clothing lay
across the foot of my bunk, consisting in part of
a pair of sailor's blue trousers, a steamer cap,
and a coat and vest of pepper-and-salt mixture,
each garment in its own humorous way contrib-
uting to the totality of a rather ludicrous misfit.
As I made my way to the gun-deck, accompanied by the stately Newfoundland, and into the
presence of her Majesty's officers, chagrin at my

personal appearance nearly overcame that more becoming sense of gratitude due to my deliverers.

I had little time or inclination to think of my losses until after I had been ashore on the following morning, and telegraphed in a roundabout way to New York for funds. First of all, and most deplorable, there were my precious negatives stowed away in the leather bag, only so many pieces of worthless glass. A clear actinic light, such as I delighted to operate in, bathed the straggling town lying under the great honeycombed rock, and sparkled on the now placid harbor where the vessels of the Channel fleet rode at anchor ; but, alas ! my camera was at the bottom of the sea. The main spars of the Utopia were just showing above the wreck, about which there was a congregation of boats, and divers were busily searching for bodies.

As I looked, later in the day, from the bridge of the Camperdown across the water to this scene of submarine industry, the thought of the scrap of paper committed to my care by Philip Coe, came for the first time to my mind, and I remembered that I had placed the envelope in the leather bag with the negatives. I would at least make an effort to rescue this property of my friend, and I turned away in search of the officer of the deck. I had no money to employ a diver for this service, but just here several of her Majesty's young officers came to my aid, and not caring myself to pay a personal visit to the ghastly scenes about the wreck, the very obliging officers despatched a messenger, to whom I furnished in writing the number of my state-room, together with the location and a description of the bag containing the negatives, which was successfully recovered.

The action of the salt-water on the envelope had been such that directly it was exposed to the sun it opened of itself, the triangular lap curling up slowly as if it had been some species of shell-fish, and to hasten the process of drying I took out the inclosure and spread it on the deck. It was simply a receipt for a package left at the office of the Astor House in New York, to be delivered to the bearer whose name was written across the sealed opening of the package aforesaid. This was the gist of the statement contained in a somewhat more elaborate printed form.

I remained on board the Camperdown just long enough to complete the process of drying, reseal the envelope, indorsed by Philip Coe, pitch my precious negatives into the sea, and all hope of triumph at the club along with them, kick the sodden bag under a gun carriage, and confer on my dog the high-sounding and warlike name of Camperdown, in return for the hospitality of her Majesty's gallant officers. The bestowal of the name was a parting impulse of gratitude which was all the return I could make for my generous entertainment and my ill-fitting clothes, and directly thereafter, Camperdown and my more insignificant self were piped over the side of her Majesty's ironclad and rowed in great state to the steamer provided by the Anchor line to convey the survivors of the wreck to Liverpool. where we should meet the Furnessia bound for New York.   .

II

AT Liverpool I found funds awaiting me in response to my telegram from Gibraltar, and as I had four days on my hands before the departure of the Furnessia, having secured my cabin I concluded to run up to London and refit. After purchasing my railway ticket I telegraphed Philip Coe of my arrival in Liverpool, and informed him that the paper he had committed to my care was still in my custody.

Every newspaper account of the loss of the Utopia had mentioned my name and that of the Newfoundland dog as the sole survivors among the cabin passengers of that ill-fated ship, and Camperdown and I were the acknowledged heroes of that newspaper week. I was satisfied that my friend was aware of my existence, and I only wished to apprise him of the safety of his bit of property.

As soon as I had inscribed my name on the register of my hotel at London the clerk handed me a telegram, and as I smoothed it out on the office counter, he remarked, with surprising loquacity for one of his kind, " That's a rawther long wire, Doctor."

The telegram *was* rather long, for a man without any luggage, and not over-well dressed at that, but it was from Coe, who was profuse in his congratulations on my safety and, with his characteristic modesty, not a word was said about the paper he had committed to my care for safe-keeping.

I have neglected to state that before leaving Liverpool I had placed Camperdown in the care of the steward on board the Furnessia, making every provision for his security and comfort. We had become such great friends, on short acquaintance, that I am free to confess that, on my part, the parting was a serious one, and as I looked into his great wondering eyes as the steward held him back by his chain, I felt that I was leaving behind a creature almost human in his affection, for whom I felt something nearer to love than I at present attached to any other man, woman, or dog in the world.

As I seated myself in my compartment of the London and Liverpool train, absolutely empty-handed, without so much as an umbrella or an extra coat, I felt the momentary shock of the man who has forgotten something : and then the absurdity of my situation, in its humorous aspect, forced itself upon me. My elaborate photographic outfit, and every change of clothing I had possessed were at the bottom of the sea, and there I sat (I stood to one side for the moment regarding my real self as an amusing outside entity of the third person), a man who would be known at sight for an American going up to London in a first-class carriage, as it were, sucking his thumbs. I felt an uncomfortable desire to clutch something, and so it came about that I wandered out to the platform and fastened to a novel to bear me company.

On my return I observed that an elderly gentleman and a young girl, evidently his daughter, had taken the opposite seat in the compartment. My first feeling was vexation at my stupidity in not having engaged the whole place for myself, as I am rather particular about my dress, and to be under the scrutiny of a handsome young woman, herself faultlessly clad, was not a situation to my liking.

Then, too, the book I had purchased proved to be a dull one, and industriously as I persisted in reading it, I was unable to exclude from my ears the conversation of my travelling companions.

They were Americans, and it soon became
evident that we should be fellow-passengers on
the Furnessia. The girl was really beautiful
without appearing to be conscious of it, but her
devotion to her father, who seemed to be ail-
ing, had about it a charm so far beyond personal comeliness that I found myself reading
page after page of my book on which my companions figured as characters against a printed
background of absolute vacuity. There was
apparently, too, a great deal more about London tailors and bootmakers in that obliging
book than the author had put there, and I se-
cretly hoped that I should not be identified
with the very correctly attired young gentleman, whom I saw in imagination on the deck
of the Furnessia, and whom I was vaguely
planning to array in sober, well - fitting gar-
ments such as would meet the approval of the
well-bred female person who sat opposite me.

I was getting on surprisingly fast, and if honest Camperdown had been aware of the state of
my mind, he would have been consumed with
jealousy. I listened to the low, musical voice
whose caressing tones clung about the girl's
silent, elderly companion, and filled the carriage with the soothing melody of a song of
home. As for my book, the tamer it got the

harder I read it. The story (between the lines) skipped over seas, from continent to continent at the will of the musical voice. It treated of the city of Charleston and of a school girl's remembrances of the great earthquake, and as the voice flowed on, the vague figures of the friends of the voice glided behind the vaguer print of the book in an entertaining panorama. I turned the page to plunge into the heart of Paris, and then travelled up into Switzerland and slid gently down to Rome (where there was just a paragraph in parenthesis about Philip Coe), and then we drifted out to sea with only one woman on the great liner, and then dropped down at the old New York Hotel just as the train rumbled into the gloom of the London station, where the yellow lamps were blinking outside in the mist.

The door of the compartment was thrown open and I found myself standing on the flagging of the station gazing after the forms of my two companions, with whom I had not exchanged a word, now rapidly fading into the fog. I must have cut a highly eccentric figure, in my semi-nautical togs, with the entertaining book open in my hand and perfectly oblivious to the bustle about me.

" Any luggage, sir ? " cried cabby.

" Yes, there's a camera and a paper."

" Whereabouts, sir ? "

" At the bottom of the Mediterranean—stateroom 59."

" See here, my man," I interrupted myself, " are you talking to me ? There's no baggage —luggage. Drive me to a hotel."

" Which one, your honor ? "

" Anyone," said I, and carefully putting the interesting book into my pocket, I sprang into the cab with a new consciousness that there was something the matter with me. And then I put out my head and designated my hotel, and so it came about that I was landed at the proper place to meet Philip Coe's telegram.

Four days, just then, was a weary time in the wilderness of London, but I pulled myself together and fought a gallant fight against large plaids and polka-dot neckerchiefs, and in the fulness of time I was trundled on board the Furnessia, with just enough boxes to render me respectable in the estimation of the steward, and into the company of Camperdown, who didn't seem to notice that I had changed a hair.

Early in the morning of this day of departure, after making a rather extravagant investment in cut roses, I had bought the florist's whole stock of potted violets, and ordered the entire purchase to be packed in boxes and delivered in my cabin on board. I was in a delightfully reckless frame of mind; had totally forgotten the lost negatives, and on the way to the docks in a cab, found myself chuckling in such an ecstasy of delight, as to put my driver in serious jeopardy of arrest for unpardonable carelessness in transporting a dangerous lunatic.

During all the bustle of departure I peered about among the crowds for a sight of my companions of the railway compartment. Somehow I had an abiding faith that the two figures, which I had seen to dissolve into the London fog, had materialized again and were somewhere stowed away on board the big liner. But it was the possibility of being mistaken in this hopeful prognosis that, for the first few days at sea, made life a nervous unsatisfactory burden, which was never so tolerable to bear as during those hours, when stretched on my berth in the seclusion of my cabin, I lent myself to the luxury of recalling the charms of that incomparable young woman from Charleston.

She was tall; of ample proportions; the picture of health; just the superb figure to house a wholesome mind; a thought blond, with abundant brown hair; large eyes as sympathetic as Camperdown's and strong, regular white teeth ; large, well-shapen hands ; a neatly fitting costume of twilled cloth, which must have been gray ; a felt hat surmounted by a bird's wing which I remembered was lavender ; three long-stemmed English roses in the corsage, one of which was half concealed by the lapel of her jacket ; and the other figure, of the old man, was strangely out of focus and imperfectly developed.

Arrived this far, my mind invariably went back to the large expressive eyes ; I heard again the musical, well-modulated voice and, in desperation, watered my flowers and turned out to walk the deck and stroll with an air of assumed unconcern into every accessible nook and cranny of the ship in search of the beautiful original.

During the first two days of the voyage the sea was choppy with a cold, drizzling rain which made the decks slippery and uninviting even to the most determined pedestrians. On the third the sun came out in all his glory, drawing a thin mist of steam from the wet cordage and the canvas coverings of the boats on the davits, and from their cabins such of the passengers as had no imperative call to remain longer in seclusion. Camperdown and I went joyfully forth to greet the sun and take our morning exercise with the rest. Our association in public led to occasional remarks along the rail, that convinced me that our newspaper notoriety of the past week was not yet forgotten. We affected not to notice this trifling distinction from which we had no means of escape, except by retiring from view altogether, and having made our way well aft I took my stand in a sheltered niche behind the boats, looking out to sea and revolving in my mind the advisability of sending Camperdown below. Without particularly noticing it, I was aware that my shaggy companion had made a new acquaintance (the ladies were very much given to petting him), and then I heard two words—only two— " Good Camperdown," in the unmistakable accents of the musical voice of the compartment of the London and Liverpool train. I turned about so suddenly and so awkwardly to confront my former fellow-passengers, that a becoming shade of confusion flitted across the handsome face which contained the large eyes and white teeth of my dreams, and then passing instantly to a state of the most perfect self-possession, she said :

" I beg your pardon, I was surprised to see the gentleman who sat opposite us going up to

London on Saturday," and then, as if to explain her greeting to Camperdown, "everybody on the ship has heard of your late adventure, and Camperdown is a great hero."

The easy frankness of her manner added a new charm to her personality, and the length of her speech gave me time to recover from the tumult of agreeable sensations with which her sudden appearance, like a sunburst out of that London fog, had fairly dazzled me. "I remember you very well," I said, bowing at the same time to the old gentleman done up in rugs, and feeling an indefinable sense that I was a monster of deception in saying so little when I felt so much.

"Won't you join us, Dr. Lattimer," said a feeble voice out of the bundle of rugs, adding something about my interesting experience, and something more about the warmth of the sun and the shelter from the wind, and at the same time introducing himself and his daughter, all of which, under the calm gaze of the young woman's eyes, was very much mixed with the throb of the engines and the beating of my heart. I sat down, however, with what I believed to be a highly triumphant victory of mind over matter, ordered Camperdown to compose himself, acknowledged my identity with the sailor-man in the railway compartment, and got back into the salt scud and the awful uncertainty of Gibraltar harbor, as what wouldn't I have done for the entertainment of the object of my secret infatuation.

It turned out to be a red letter morning. I succeeded in getting our whole party into the highest of spirits, including Mr. Dangerking, who laughed quietly in his wraps, and otherwise left the field to his lovely daughter. He was altogether such a dear old gentleman that I counted myself fortunate to be allowed to carry down his wraps, and incidentally mentioning that my friends had been unusually lavish in their floral contributions, in one burst of gratitude I sent him my whole stock of cut roses.

I was in for it! I knew I was in for it. If the Utopia had not gone to the bottom, I should have returned to a blighted and aimless life. I am thirty, and I was perfectly aware that I was behaving like a boy of seventeen, and the worst of it all was I exulted in my folly.

I rejoined that young woman in the afternoon, on deck, a bunch of blush roses — my roses—peeping from the breast of her ulster, and we struggled against the wind as against a common enemy ; and I thought of the arm I had thrown over Camperdown in a similar extremity, and noted the resemblance of Miss Dangerking's eyes to Camperdown's when I first met him in that scudding sea.

Miss Dangerking was something of a hero worshipper, and she usually insisted upon Camperdown being one of the party, " for chaperon, you know," and I felt that I had advanced many degrees in her approval by virtue of my peculiar experience. She consulted me in regard to her father's health with a confidence which was altogether charming, and at the request of that gentleman I was installed at his private table, and on the very first occasion when we sat down together, a mysterious vase of fresh violets ornamented the centre of the board. Now violets, being the most perishable of flowers, their presence on this occasion in dewy freshness, four days out from Liverpool, was just a little short of a miracle, and the wonderment they excited was the first-fruit of my foresight on embarking. I advised Miss Dangerking to wear them as freely as if fresh violets grew on the cross-trees, trusting me to replace these with fresher ones in the morning.

My patient, if I may call him such, slept regularly in the afternoon, and when the weather was favorable Miss Dangerking and I, attended by Camperdown, spent that part of the day on deck. I was never so happy as when my companion was recounting with girlish frankness some event in her life, and I was permitted to lie back in my chair and gaze, a respectful listener, into those unfathomable eyes and note the changes of expression flitting across her mobile face. That there was some trouble casting its baleful shadow there, other than the trouble caused by her father's illness, I felt by instinct, but the only acknowledged secret between us was the mystery of the fresh violets.

It was the last evening we were to spend on board, and something of the balm of the first week in April had come out to us on the west wind ; and we made our way aft and arranged our chairs where we could look back along the white track of the steamer as it lay a furrow of foam over the gentle swells.

Our perfectly frank and natural association on the voyage now closing had ripened into a richer fruit, which I trembled at the thought of plucking, lest by some unlucky wind its fragrance should be scattered forever. The future is always full of doubt. Our mood— mine at least—was retrospective, and so it fell

out, that we sat for a long time in silence looking back on the trail of the ship, the spark of
my cigar just showing in the gloom. Miss
Dangerking's chair was a trifle in advance so
that her figure was relieved against that part of
the sky where the moon was rising.

A deeper breath, which may or may not have
been a sigh, a relaxing of lines, and the mass
of Miss Dangerking's head turned in my direction. I knew that the invisible eyes rested full
on mine. For a moment I was silent under
the sweet influence of that gaze, only indicated,
on her part, by the action of her head.

" Our passage is drawing to an end." (I.)

" Yes." (She.)

At the sound of our voices, Camperdown
made his appearance out of the gloom where he
had been sleeping, and, but for my restraint,
would have licked the hand which lay so
quietly on the arm of Miss Dangerking's
chair.

As I have remarked before, I am not given
to hesitation when the time for action comes.
I extended my hand and laid it firmly on that
other hand so white in the moonlight, with
perfect confidence in my ability to speak. For
the first time in my life the words left me. I
felt a tremor in the long fingers under mine.

I choked and stammered, and only managed to say, "Miss Dangerking, you know——"

I was not frightened in the sense of being terrified, but this time I had essayed a plunge without being prepared for it. If that other plunge over the side of the Utopia had been half as terrible, I should have gone down never to rise again.

"Miss—Miss Dangerking——"

The under hand had ceased to tremble, and the tone of my voice was beginning to assert itself.

"Please don't, Dr. Lattimer, we are so happy as we are."

Did ever man obey such an injunction at such a time? A half-hour afterward I was sitting alone in the same place, as a consequence of my reckless disobedience, smoking violently, and gazing out to sea in a vain endeavor to determine whether I was partly happy or utterly miserable. Some things had happened which put my head in a whirl to remember, but Miss Dangerking had insisted that everything was impossible, and it was when I begged to speak to her father that, with strange agitation, she had entreated me to come to her, at their hotel on the following evening, for an explanation.

III

I ARRIVED promptly at the hour appointed, and was shown into the presence of Miss Dangerking. She gave me her hand unreservedly, motioned me to a seat opposite her, and with a perceptibly heightened color mantling her handsome face, proceeded directly to the subject of the interview.

"You know my feelings toward you, Dr. Lattimer," she said, with the most engaging candor. For a moment her eyes fell as if in deep thought, and then she continued : "The causes which have led to my father's broken condition you are ignorant of. It is on that subject I feel it my duty to enlighten you.

"My father is resting under grave charges of the misappropriation of the funds of an estate committed to his care as a banker. He has twice stood trial—twice been convicted, and he is returning now to surrender himself for trial in the court of last resort — with the ablest counsel in the State to defend him—but with no new evidence, although the attorneys have sought for it diligently. The trust consisted of a very large sum in Government bonds and railway shares, and three days before the final accounting was called for, the securities were safe in my father's private vault. There was no trace of a robbery ; no one connected with the bank disappeared ; there was no clerk to whom the slightest taint of suspicion could attach. With my father's nice sense of honorable dealing he would never consent to the engagement you have proposed. It is because I wished to spare him the pain of such a decision that I determined to make this explanation myself."

The extreme youth of the speaker, the cool business statement she had made of the salient points in a case at law, with none of the protestations or bewailings which most girls would have bestowed upon such a narrative, invested her with a womanly dignity that would have won my admiration if I had never seen her before. The uncomplaining devotion with which, on a long foreign journey, Miss Dangerking had reversed the order of nature, becoming the protector of her natural protector, had already captivated my imagination, and as I have admitted before, I was past the stage of reason.

" I do not believe a word of those charges

against your father," I said, springing to my feet.

Miss Dangerking rose and extended her hand, her beautiful eyes swimming with gratitude.

" Come and see us every day if you will, but never speak of our relations, and never mention in my father's presence the subject of this interview."

A cold April rain was pelting the windows when I took my departure. Countless lances of light were stabbing the stones of the street. A dreary chorus of fog-horns sounded from the rivers. The windows of the carriage streamed with the rain, reminding me of the bulls-eyes of the Utopia before that vessel grounded on the iron ram of the Anson.

Of the fearful consequences of a final conviction, Miss Dangerking had said not a word. I was enjoined from pressing my suit. I determined to devote all my energies to the discovery of the missing evidence, which was another indication that my love had dethroned my reason; I knew it and exulted in it. If trained lawyers had failed to find the missing link, what would a medical expert be likely to accomplish? I did not choose to accept the logical deduction of my own hypothesis. I was determined to butt my stupid, infatuated head against the

stone wall of the law. Accordingly I placed
myself in communication with the counsel for
the defence in the case of the People vs. Dangerking, and in due time was in possession of
the numbers and issues of the Government bonds
and a complete description of the railroad securities.

Miss Dangerking accepted my attention to
her father's health and my devotion to herself
with a perfect understanding of the spirit in
which they were offered, and, on my part, I was
entirely loyal to the injunction she had placed
upon the expression of my wishes in a certain
direction. She resumed her former frank,
cheerful manner, as if no gulf of impending disaster yawned under her feet. It was impossible
to regard her as a girl. The only girlish trait
she showed was an extravagant fondness for
Camperdown, and the two certainly made a
stately and distinguished appearance together
on the streets, and would never have been separated at all if the railway officials had shared
my views of the dog's rights in the matter of a
first-class ticket by the Charleston limited.

A fortnight later, I had accomplished absolutely nothing in diagnosing the case of the
People vs. Dangerking. The missing securities
showed no symptoms of responding to my

method of treatment. I had not even evolved a plausible diagnosis to begin on. Offensive as the act was to my professional instincts, in sheer desperation, I inserted a description of the missing property through an advertising agency, in an extended list of newspapers, both in the United States and Canada, offering a liberal reward for information. I craved the advice and assistance of a cool head, such as reposed on the shoulders of Philip Coe. I had an impulse to send for him. Even if I had possessed his address I had no right to demand such a sacrifice of a casual acquaintance, and no reason to believe that such a request would be complied with. It was plainly a whim too wild for my excited imagination to entertain seriously, and I put it out of my thoughts.

What could I do to ward off the fatal result in the approaching trial of my amiable and innocent patient, and the crushing blow of an adverse verdict to the woman I loved ? Besides torturing me by day, the subject was robbing me of sleep by night. I could go to Charleston and consult with the defendant's counsel. It would be a relief to know from day to day just what was being done in the case. It was June now, and Miss Dangerking and her father were absent from the already hot city. I could devote myself all the more assiduously to my investigation if only a clue could be found to work on.

On the afternoon of the day before my intended departure for Charleston I was sitting in my office, more cast down than ever, having but just returned from a long and fruitless consultation with the chief of police. In fact I was nearer to the point where a man yields to cowardly despair than I had ever before had occasion to be. Even Camperdown gave over his amiable attempts to arouse me and stalked away to his private quarters in the back office. The windows were open onto the quiet cross street. The China silk curtains hung limp and motionless in the still hot air, and outside the insects droned and buzzed in the muggy heat despite the absence of their friend the sun, whose rays were quenched in a thin, sticky mist of impalpable fog.

A solitary cab rattled over the pavement, its unwelcome clatter magnified fourfold in the drowsy stillness. It pulled up with a lurch unpleasantly suggestive of a fever patient tossing in some gilded apartment, and the arrested horse continued to stamp his inconsiderate feet on the hot stones.

The door which stood ajar swung inward.

A breezy figure projected itself against the light.

"How's the amateur photographer? Not mourning over those water-logged negatives? Hey, Doctor?"

"Mourning over nothing, my dear Coe," I cried, "except the heat."

"Heat! Come now—don't say heat to a man fresh from Algeria. Air feels rather frosty this morning. Sun just stopped short of melting my plates in that African bake-shop. I hung around the engine on the steamer and suffered with the cold like a February gosling. I've found a climate just suited to my blood."

"You didn't go to Russia?"

"No. Sudden attack of home-sickness."

"Glad of it. You're the very man I wanted to see. You've cleared the atmosphere like a gust of wind already. Come in this morning? So—I want to consult you in an emergency."

"Well, why not, Doctor, you own me for the present. Hello! Is that the dog from Gibraltar? Devilish fine dog—What's—his—name—Camperdown? Do you know, I've had a prejudice against dogs from a child. And that splendid brute knows it. How do you account for it?"

Sure enough Camperdown growled and showed his teeth, a thing that I had never seen him do before, and for which I promptly ordered him out of our presence.

Philip Coe sat down and insisted on having the particulars of my shipwreck, only interrupting me with an occasional question or an ejaculation of satisfaction over my perseverance and final rescue. "And your last will and testament, by the way," I said, going over to the safe and extracting the envelope la padrona had given us in the Trattorea Fiorelli, "here you are."

"Oh! I'm glad you mentioned it," said Philip Coe, placing it in his breast pocket. "It's enough for the present that you got your own precious skin out of the brine."

"You must dine with me to-night," I said, "and we will talk over the matter to which I referred—something that is disturbing me very much at present, sorry to say—(I saw that he was moving to go)—meet me here at seven, then."

The horse that had never ceased to stamp at the flies, now rattled away over the pavement.

The color of the world had changed since the advent of my resourceful friend, and I congratulated myself on his timely arrival. I was not content to enjoy the fact alone, and, seizing a pen, lover-like, I wrote a brief note to Miss Dangerking, predicting hopeful results from the opportune arrival of Philip Coe. I took Camperdown out for a walk, revolving in my mind how I should present the all-absorbing case to my shrewd friend, remembering that his judgment was not influenced by any sympathy for my patient, and having a fear that he would pronounce a sharp and incisive opinion that the defendant was guilty as charged.

It was half-past five when Philip Coe left my office. It still wanted a half-hour of the time set for dinner when he returned. He tossed a package onto the table, wrapped in a strong, gray paper, showing two red seals. He was evidently in some new hurry. The instant he laid his package down I noticed that his name was written diagonally across the wrapper between the seals. I recognized it as the package from the Astor House.

" Business is business, my dear Doctor," he explained, as soon as he had recovered his breath, and wiping his wrists with his handkerchief as he spoke,—" awfully sorry, but I have to leave for St. Louis by an early train. Haven't time to cut off my coupons. I was getting short of money, and that is the real

reason of my return. Expected to have plenty
of time to shear my flock and realize on the
wool to-morrow.''

"But, my dear fellow, you forget that I pos-
itively can't spare you—I want to use you—I
need your advice.''

"Give it to you at dinner, but go I must—
telegram imperative.''

"When can you come back?''

"I will be in New York again in a week at
the farthest,'' said Philip Coe, "and then we'll
develop my negatives together,'' laying his hand
on my shoulder and brightening at the joyful
prospect.

"If you need any money, say so,'' said I.

"Money,'' cried he, tapping the package
which lay on the table. "I'm loaded with
money. You shall turn in and help me cut
coupons after dinner. It's because I shall want
a considerable sum on Saturday that I propose
to pick these birds to-night and ask you to de-
posit the proceeds to your own account and
mail me a check. That's not much to ask of a
friend,'' he rattled on, severing the cord and
breaking the seals of the package.

I naturally felt an extraordinary interest in
the contents of a parcel the receipt for which
had accompanied me through so many advent-

ures, but I only looked on in respectful silence.

Philip Coe was bent over at his work under the glare of the drop-light. I stood above and behind him, a little withdrawn from the heat of the gas.

"There," said he, laying out a thousand dollar Government 4 of 1907, "it will be short work and merry. I haven't seen the smiling faces of these fellows in over a year."

It was a mercy that my face was removed from the scrutiny of Philip Coe. It must have blanched with a tell-tale pallor for an instant, for my blood seemed to stand still and the room swam before my astonished eyes as I noted the issue and number of the bond.

He continued to look through the package hurriedly, turning out paper after paper as if to satisfy himself that the contents had not been disturbed in his absence, and in the brilliant light I too read the name of the very railway securities which were missing in the case of the People *vs.* Dangerking, and began to realize the cool villany of the man, who had so skilfully played with my confidence.

My maid servant appeared at the door.

"Dinner is served, my dear boy," I cried. "Put that lumber in the safe until we have eaten something."

With the most perfect confidence in his victim he replaced the papers, closed the wrapper loosely over the package and laid his booty carefully on the steel shelf I designated (the door of the safe had stood open since I had taken out the envelope containing his receipt), and I closed the combination.

At the soft click of that oily lock as the massive bolts slid smoothly into place over the missing evidence in the case of the People *vs.* Dangerking, my spirits rose and my brain was as clear and cool as a chess-player's who sees mate in the next move.

"I don't know how you feel, old fellow," said I, clapping Philip Coe heartily on the shoulder, "but I am as hungry as a hound," and I led the way briskly to the dining-room.

"I'm still in possession of my sea appetite," said he, as he seated himself opposite to me and shook out his napkin.

The table was a round one reduced to its smallest dimensions, so that we could easily have shaken hands across it if we had been so disposed.

Although my mind was acting in a twofold capacity it in nowise interfered with the relish and vivacity with which we addressed ourselves to the dinner. Hospitality under the circum-

stances rose to the dignity of a fine art—as fine
as the edge of a lancet.

" Do you remember the last time we drank
Asti Spumanti together? " I cried, as I
loosened the napkin-muffled cork.

"Well, rather," said Philip Coe, settling
back in his chair with a comfortable reminiscent
laugh. " I can see the green light between
those vine-frescoed walls and smell the fruity
casks piled upon the earthen floor."

" And I," said I, " inhale the atmosphere
of la padrona at this moment, as she brought
us the envelope for your document," and I
smiled meaningly over at the man who had so
cunningly made use of me to transport and
protect a compromising paper which he feared
to carry on his own person.

" By the way," said I, " —a—Mary " (she
was removing the remains of the fish) " is
William in the house? " and then to Coe,
" We shall want some cigars presently, and I
am going to send my boy out for something
that will give you a genuine surprise, old
smoker that you are."

As I said this I produced a blank prescrip-
tion pad and wrote as follows :

" I am dining at this moment with a man

whom you want. Post two officers opposite my
door at once."

"J. Q. LATTIMER, M.D.

"——— Gramercy Park."

"Do you like them strong?" I asked, looking up at my guest.

"Not too strong," he replied, "anything
that suits you will suit me."

I wondered if it would. I felt a wave of
shame at having indulged in such cruel badi-
nage. I tore off the paper from the pad,
doubled it carefully, wrote on the outside :

" Inspector———
Mulberry Street,"

took a banknote from my pocket, laid it over
the address, and handed it to Mary with instructions to give it to William.

"That potted pigeon isn't half bad, is it?"
said I ; "let me fill your glass. Take your
time, enjoy yourself to the utmost. After we
get on to the dessert I want to consult you
about my affair. You haven't told me anything yet about your luck in Algeria."

Philip Coe was in such a charming humor
that he launched directly into his African ex-

periences, which were sufficiently entertaining
and so delightfully told that I felt a conviction
that he might have been equally successful as
an author, without being a plagiarist either.

I had abundant time to consider what I
should say when my turn came, for we were
still on the subject of Algeria when the coffee
was served.

Fortunately I had an unopened box of cigars
in the butler's pantry, and as we were now left
. alone I fetched the box myself and opened it
on the table.

Since I had proposed to take counsel of
Philip Coe, such a revolution had taken place
in my feelings toward the man who sat opposite
to me, that I had no longer the faintest need
of his advice. I had offered my hospitality to
a personal friend in whom I had the utmost
confidence; in a moment he had been transformed into a cunning, designing, treacherous
enemy. Whether he was principal or confederate in the robbery, the evidence of which
he had so strangely laid before me, I had no
means of knowing. I was not yet ready to
accuse him of a crime. It was not a pleasant
or a courteous proceeding when the culprit was
at the same time the honored guest at my table.
I shrank from seeming to be rude. If I opened

my heart to him frankly, as I had at first intended to do, relating the story of my love and
then reciting in order the difficulties which prevented my engagement to Miss Dangerking,
the innocent story, itself, would be the accuser.
I therefore decided to place myself behind the
story and watch its effects on Philip Coe, who
at the moment was complacently inhaling the
fragrance of his cigar as innocent of what was
passing in my mind as the roses which exhaled
their delicate perfume over the space that lay
between us.

I confessed that the story I was about to relate was a story of love, and then I entered into
the minutest details of that journey up to
London, expatiating on the beauty of the fair
unknown, and not forgetting to describe my
grotesque dress and my bewildered condition
in the foggy station.

I could see that my guest was deeply interested. He rallied me on my infatuation.
He laughed at my humorous points with that
joyous abandon with which a man laughs after
dinner. As I told him of my love for this
girl, taking him into my confidence to a greater
degree than I have taken the reader, he grew
quite sympathetic.

" Devilish fine girl," he cried, " and she's

fond of you too, Doctor. Don't you give her up——"

" I never give up anything I get my hands on," said I. " Coe, that's a peculiarity of mine."

" Fine scene that in the moonlight," said he, filling his glass. " And she gave you no reason for her refusal ? "

" Oh, yes, she did," said I. " Her father was charged with a crime — embezzling the funds of a trust or something of that sort. She told me herself like a martyr, rather than subject him to pain.

" Did she, though ? " said Philip Coe, starting forward into an attitude of enthusiastic admiration. " Lattimer, that girl is a thoroughbred. I'm half in love with her myself. She is an American through and through. And then raising his tiny glass in his fingers, " Let us drink the health of Miss——"

" Dangerking," I suggested, " from Charleston."

His eyes flashed on mine. His cold face changed color for an instant, but his hand holding the brimming glass was without a sign of tremor. " Marry her, my dear fellow," he said. " She is worthy of you. Her health——"

" Wait a moment." I said ; " the suspicion

that attaches to her father can only be removed
by the discovery of the securities he is charged
with having taken. Those securities, Philip
Coe," I said, rising and pointing my finger at
my guest. " Those securities——"

" Are locked in your strong box. Pray be
seated, Dr. Lattimer. Any heat on your part
is most unbecoming at this time. As your
guest, I would save you from marring your
hospitality with the slightest rudeness. We
evidently understand each other. Let us ad-
journ to your office and talk this matter over
calmly."

Philip Coe led the way and I followed in
silence, thankful that he had saved me from any
further elaboration of my charges. Arrived in
my office, he faced about and addressed me as
follows :

" You have won some distinction, Dr. Lattimer, in the practice of your profession ; a
condition I carefully avoid in the practice of
mine. We both regard advertising as highly
unprofessional. We will waive the fact that I
have been dining at your table. Without
further waste of words, Dr. Lattimer, I shall
trouble you to return me the package I handed
you before dinner. I am prepared to enforce
my demand."

We were both standing; the table with its
shaded lamp between us, and as Philip Coe
made his demand he thrust his hand behind him
with a motion which I perfectly understood.

The next instant a gleaming revolver was
pointed at my head. I mildly suggested that
the secret of the combination which held the
package he wanted was known to me alone.
"What would be the advantage to you of adding murder," I said, "to the already long
list of your crimes?"

A malignant gleam of hatred shot from his
evil eyes. I remembered the cool precision
with which he levelled his camera and the admirable prudence that governed the drop of his
shutter. He was not the man to waste a plate
or a bullet.

The curtain rustled in the faint evening
breeze, making the only sound in the lighted
room since I had ceased to speak.

"Close that window, Dr. Lattimer," was
the only reply he made to my remonstrance. I
turned to the window. The two officers I had
summoned were leaning against a lamp-post on
the opposite side of the street. The light fell
full on them. They were looking directly
across. No unusual sound or movement could
escape their observation.

" Before I close this window," said I, " let me call your attention to those two figures over the way," and I drew the curtains aside sufficiently to give him an uninterrupted view. " They are awaiting a sign or a motion from me."

He made no reply, but the hand holding the weapon was lowered. I no longer feared him.

" Sit down, Philip Coe," said I. "Instead of sending for cigars an hour ago, I sent for those gentlemen. It is not necessary for them to observe us further at present."

I drew the curtains together.

" You are a remarkable man, Dr. Lattimer. You buy out florists, and summon police officers with equal foresight. Would you mind throwing this dangerous weapon in your wastepaper basket? "

I did precisely as he requested me.

" I know when I am beaten," he said, seating himself at the table. He bit off the end of a cigar, lighted it, and passed it under his nose as if to assure himself of its quality. I couldn't help admiring his cool self-possession. Critical as the situation was, my remarkable guest showed no signs of fear, no agitation, no excitement. He was perfectly calm and collected. With his faculty for quick mental combinations, he recognized the jaws of the trap which held him. He was evidently a philosopher of the school of fatalists.

"I am rather fond of my liberty," said Philip Coe, pushing about some bits of paper on the table with his long flexible fingers. "You have taken possession of the fruits of my last speculation! My arrival, unfortunate as it has been to myself, clears your friends, and opens the way to your uttermost happiness. What do you propose to offer me in return for this?"

The hint at my happiness was an overwhelming appeal. On the threshold of the joyful future made possible by the happenings of this eventful night I shrank from being the cause of further sufferings to the principal agent in the new turn of affairs.

"Clear up the mystery connected with this robbery," I said, perfectly aware that I was compounding a felony, "and you shall depart as freely as you came. As to your friends over the way, I will tell them it was all a mistake."

His explanation covered everything, even to the odd circumstance of leaving the valuable package for so long a time in the keeping of the authorities of the hotel. An officer of the law had been hot on his trail for another offence, and to elude pursuit he had dodged on board an outgoing steamer, carrying with him the receipt which I had been at so much pains to bring back for him.

After this statement had been written out by his own hand, I called in the waitress who had served us at dinner to witness the signature. The name attached to the document was Philip Coe, the same which had appeared in the paper I had dried out on the deck of the Camperdown, and which was written across the opening of the broken package in my safe.

One afternoon in the autumn, Miss Dangerking and I, with Camperdown in close attendance, were pacing slowly to and fro on the shady side of Lafayette Place over against the sombre front of the Astor Library, and along that colonnade of Corinthian columns of a departed glory, which she called a gallery, getting inexpressible comfort out of the fusted old street, and our undisturbed possession of it, and daring at last to look frankly into the clarified future. Our marriage was set for that day week.

"You have never cleared up the mystery of those wonderfully fresh violets," said Miss

Dangerking, with an earnestness I was no longer capable of trifling with.

" I sent a conservatory on board in pots at Liverpool. I thought you might like them."

"I did like them," she said, after we had walked on to a little distance, raising her sympathetic eyes from the broken flagging through which a distorted root was struggling to force its way into the light. " I was thinking of a later evidence of your thoughtfulness. I am glad that our perfect happiness is not clouded by the sense of having consigned to prison the burglar who was instrumental in bringing it about."

" The Demented Ones "

BEYOND the near hills, and veiled by the smoking woods, the battle is joined.

It is hard to say whether the roar of the artillery is heavier than the ceaseless tear and grind, grind, grind of the multitudinous rifles. High up in the murky sky the on-lookers at the rear see soft flashes of light burst into puffs of white-gray smoke. The white-curtained ambulances wax thicker and thicker on the dusty road. Wounded men, supported by one and sometimes by three comrades who have thrown away their guns, are streaming back through the woods. Here and there a riderless horse is plunging madly across the withered and stony pastures, or cropping a mouthful of grass, and then turning a startled look in the direction whence he came. Down the 'pike thunders an aid in search of re-enforcements, his smoking mount gray with dust and flecked with foam. Past him gallops a yellow-striped orderly on his way to the front, with buff envelopes drawn through his belt. A disabled gun has been hauled back on to the road-side, and the excited drivers are riding the smoking teams to the rear. Covered wagons are paying out telegraph wire over short poles driven into the earth, as they come trending in the direction of army headquarters.

There is grim order, however, in the seeming confusion. The forge is ablaze in the shabby bivouac of Battery Q's impedimenta, and the leather-aproned smith is shaping a shoe for one of the extra horses. There is the round-topped battery wagon, the little mess wagon loaded with tents and camp chairs, and the big covered van, with six kicking mules fighting over the trough fixed on the pole. And there is Uncle Moses, now lamming and cursing his charges, and now talking to them as if they were intelligent members of his family.

" Yo' low-down white Lize, lemme see yo' kick dat line mule one time moah, an' yo' Unc' Mose ull curry yo' down wid dis yer black-snake. Does yo' year me? Whoa! 'Bang! Swish!' I mek yo' squat down an' t'ank de Lor' I di'n't cut yo' heart out dat time. Whoa! "

The burly quartermaster is strutting up and down, big with the importance of his independent command, and proud of his indifference to

the roar of the battle. He is swearing more
than the occasion calls for—this quartermaster
who said his prayers and read his Bible night
and morning in a top bunk of the Albany bar-
racks when he thought he was going to certain
death, he and his devout bedfellow, who has long
since deserted.

Certainly the quartermaster is sore tried on
these peculiar occasions, when, excepting the
smith and the farrier and Uncle Moses and the
colored servants and a disabled recruit more or
less, his command is made up of idiots and
mild lunatics, thrust into the army as costly
substitutes, and unloaded on Battery Q,
along with better men, with the occasional
forced details from the infantry.

These merry freaks, first or last, found their
righteous water-level in the spavined train of the
extra horses.

Charley Fitch, with his forage - cap pulled
down until his ears lop under the rim, is seated
under the battery wagon to shelter his bare
back from the sun. Fitch stammered so badly
when he spoke that his mouth drew around
toward his left ear and his right shoulder
twitched.

Spence Lusk, his comrade in adversity, who
was sitting near him, looked on at the rising

smoke calmly, for he was deaf. He only heard
when the horse-doctor punched him in the ribs,
and then, knowing that something was being said
to him, he said, " Yes." If the doctor shook his
head, Spence hastened to say, " No, marm."
If that did not appear to satisfy the doctor,
Spence swore mildly and said, " I dun'no'."
And he was otherwise so slow in his movements that he was known throughout the battery as " Old By-and-by."

These two were drawn to each other by the
common heritage of infirmities, and Charley
took Spence under his protection with a great
show of patronage and a comfortable assumption
of superiority. Fifty times a day Charley forgot that Spence was deaf, and after saying something that twisted his whole body in the effort,
he would look at Spence despairingly, and add,
with another contortion, " Well, you no good
anyway, 'Pence Lul-lul-lusk."

It was pathetic to see these two friends without any friends, each mounted on a galled
horse of many sores, hung with festoons of
camp kettles and nose-bags, each leading two
other lame or otherwise disabled animals, deco-
rated with rolls of blankets and strings of pots
and pans. The two wore their overcoats in
August, and patiently carried every bag and

burden the men chose to strap on their horses.
In camp they cleaned and fed each his three
charges, and for the rest of the day they ate and
slept, and at night they crept under the same
dog-tent.

After feed - time Charley sidled over to
Spence, and pulling him by the shoulder,
shouted in his ear :

" There's a big hors-pi-pi-pitile down by the
sta-sta-straw-stacks.   Common ! "

" Hain't got any," said Spence, who
thought Charley was asking for tobacco.

" You ain't no good," said Charley, plucking
him by the arm, and away the two friends went
together.

The writhing of Charley's body showed that
he was making another fruitless effort to com-
municate some sort of good news to his companion, and then he caught him by the arm,
and after pulling him to a halt, made a saw of
his right hand, and worked it across Spence's
leg.   After that effort at pantomime both men
galloped off in great glee.

The straw-stacks were in a rude stable-yard
enclosed by a high wall, and on the peak of the
great red barn floated a square of yellow bunting.   Clean yellow straw lay thick on the wide
floors, and in the stables, and over the bottom

of the empty bays. The whole barn-yard was strewn with it.

When the two demented ones dodged under the wheels of the ambulances unloading at the double gates, the space in the barn was already tenanted by a ghastly company, and the busy bearers were laying the wounded and the dying in long straight rows across the yard. They looked in on the great barn floor. A tent fly had been staked out over the south doors to ward off the sun. The two demented ones were bewildered and speechless in the presence of the gory spectacle their eyes rested on. The frightened swallows were flying about under the great roof, and shining particles of dust were floating in the lances of light streaming through the cracks in the dark siding, and lying tenderly across the forms of the dead and the grimy and blood - stained faces of the living. Some sat up with crimson and white handkerchiefs about their heads, and others bent over their wounded limbs. The doctors were roughly probing for bullets, and there were wailings and cursing and laughter ringing up to the rafters. A peculiar rattling sound reached the ears of Charley. Here at his feet lay a sight that held him with a horrible fascination. It was the wounded form of a boy who would never see

again, his face shattered beyond recognition,
and in his delirium his restless hands were twisting and twisting and twisting a thin wisp of
broken straws.

" Common, Spence," said Charley, plucking
the other by the arm ; and they picked their
way out among the rows of the wounded, the
two demented ones vaguely conscious that by
some mysterious transformation they were rich
and prosperous where all their fellows were poor
and needy.

Some occult influence seemed to hold the two
in the radius of the horrors they would fain flee
from, and once out of the yard, their feet turned
around the barn to the shade of the butternut-
trees, where the surgeons in threes were plying
their horrible trade.   They stood at a distance
outside the barricade of fanning - mills and
sheep-racks blinking in the hot sun.

" Them fellers don't feel nothin'," said
Spence, meaning the anæsthetized subjects on
the tables.

"Guess I know th-a-a-at," said Charley,
writhing and twisting.   " Common ; " and he
led the willing Spence across the field to another hospital, straw-strewn. under the shade of
a great oak in the quiet pasture.

On the eastern border of this circle of the

unfortunate, where the shadow of the tree was
creeping out over them on to the field beyond,
was a little patch of Confederates, lying by
themselves, and in front of these the two wanderers stopped to contemplate the greatest
curiosity they had yet seen. There was one, a
handsome Virginia boy, his tooth-brush woven
through the button-holes of his gray jacket, who
held his canteen out to Charley, and begged
him, " for Christ's sake," to fill it with water.

Charley took the curious thick canteen of uncovered tin from the soldier's hand, and passing it to Spence, pointed in the direction of the
spring. Then he kneeled down beside the suf-
ferer and undid his roll of blankets, adjusting
them under his head and about his wounded
arm. Charley kept Spence going to and from
the spring until every man Jack of the enemy
was supplied with water.

" You are very kind," said the Virginian.

" 'That ain't no-n-nothin'," twisted Charley.

" What is your regiment ? "

" 'Tain't no r-r-regiment ; it's jis Battery Q."

" Battery Q ? " said the Southron. " Why,
I was wounded in front of Battery Q, and borne
through its guns to the ambulance. A tall
captain, black beard, Russian shoulder - knots
on his riding-jacket——"

" Yas," said Charley; " that's Captain Ne-Neal."

"Captain Neal," said the other. " Yes; he gave me a drink from his flask. The batteries were not engaged; it was the infantry; the trees were too thick. Great God ! " said he, thoughtfully; "if those two batteries should open on each other at a hundred yards ! "

Then, addressing himself to Charley and Spence, in view of their patent infirmities, he asked if they were soldiers.

" No; not ezactly," said Charley. " I'm a sub-sta-ta-ta-tute, an' he ain't no good; he's deef. We take care o' extra horses."

The wounded Virginian was more uneasy in mind than in body; for, as it transpired from his conversation with the friend who lay beside him, he was to have been married within the month. He could wait, if only she knew that he was alive and well, with only an arm to lose. " If I could only get word to Bob "— that was his brother. Many other things transpired, for the prisoners talked unreservedly in the presence of the demented ones, who sat on the ground beside them.

" Yes, I was to have been married next Sunday a week, to the sweetest girl in Falmouth County. It will break her heart if she hears I am dead. If I could step across and tell Bob how the land lies, all would be right. I would be willing to come back. But for the awful uncertainty about my life or death, I could roll over and go to sleep."

" Poor boy and poor girl ! " thought Charley.

Then the two prisoners fell to comparing the incidents of their capture.

" Mine," said the Virginian, " was about the most curious thing that ever happened, and quite the most unexpected. My brother, Bob Chew, commands our battery, tangled up in this infernal wilderness, and just in the front of this Battery Q. You could sling a cat across but for the jungle of trees. I walked out into a cart track just south of the right gun, not a team's length away, and was pulling dewberries out of the grass, when I got a volley out of a clear sky, and two infantry men ran me down that grassy road beside the stone wall ; and before I realized where I was, I was rushed through the guns of this same Battery Q. And here I am, and here I must stay—Lew Chew, a prisoner."

Charley blinked and writhed his shoulders, and made an involuntary face at Spence ; but with all his outward infirmity he possessed a singularly retentive memory. He made no combinations, formulated no plans, but the picture of the brother in command of his battery in front of Battery Q was fixed in his clouded mind, and the name of Captain Chew rang in his ears—*Bob Chew !* Sympathy for the wounded brother Lew had also taken hold of Charley. He only knew that he felt sorry and queer, and the writhing of his body and the twitching of his face were the unconscious outward evidence of a half - conscious inward state. Spence heard nothing, saw little, comprehended less.

When the two returned to the camp of the impedimenta, it was to find their great commander, the Napoleon of quartermaster - sergeants, vaporing and swearing. He too had just returned, not from the rear, but from the front, " by ——, sir ! " From the front, where Battery Q had covered itself with glory, and the officers (what remained of them) had sent back for hot coffee.

" And where is the cook to make it, and who is to carry it up ? Where are the d—— officers' slaves ? A smotherin' th'ir woolly heads under some hay-stack ; or, more like, buried in swamp mud, drawin' th'ir breath through a section of stove-pipe." He declared he would shoot them on the edge of their return. " Charley, come here. What do you know? Hold your tongue ! Saddle your horse. Silence, and do as I tell you."

Exeunt Charley and his patron saint. Enter the quartermaster and horse-doctor with a kettle of coffee.

In the middle distance is Charley seated on a bony gray horse ; Charley's shoulders and the gray's rump plentifully sprinkled with chopped hay and chaff. The two straps of his overcoat hang loose from the small of his back, and his elongated forage-cap is crushed down, like a drunken extinguisher, far below his turned-up coat collar. A nose-bag full of curry-combs is buckled around the neck of the patient horse, and a festoon of canteens and frying-pans deco-rates the cantle of the saddle.

The road is filled with batteries and ammu-nition wagons going and coming, so that our humble purveyors of coffee take to the fields, riding Indian file and in Indian silence, the sergeant, scowling, in advance, and Charley turning his head from side to side. In one di-rection he seeks a park of pontoon boats ad-vanced into the shelter of the woods ; and in the other the commanding general, at the head of a bedraggled staff, returning from a personal inspection of the lines.

All is still at the front, and seemingly motionless, until they pass the first curtain of woods,
and come suddenly upon countless masses of
infantry marching with an easy swing to the
left. The batteries are choking the sandy
cross - roads. No drums, no bugles, only the
jangle of equipments, the shucking of wheels,
and the rattle of harness; a quiet command,
a ribald joke, a ringing oath. Two corps are
swinging from right to left in preparation for a
new attack at daylight.

"Are we going to the f-f-front?" Charley
ventured to ask.

" Yes ; to be shot," was the sergeant's surly
rejoinder.

And on they push as before, through and beyond the moving columns. And here is the
position of Battery Q, facing the green wall of
a tangled wood at a hundred feet interval, with
guns double-shotted with canister; a battalion
of infantry, lounging in two detachments about
stacked arms behind either flank, kindling fires
of twigs and stubble to boil the everlasting quart-
cup. The numbers about the guns are lounging and even sleeping near their places. The
lids of the green limbers are closed, and the
thirsty horses are going back in teams of sixes
for water. It is an anomalous situation for a

long-range battery. A few men and horses
have gone down during the long day before the
hissing bullets now and then singing over the
field from distant sharp - shooters, or spitting
through the trees from the positions of the
skirmishers. Not a shot has been fired by the
black guns, and the duty of the support has
been a sinecure of idleness, a tedious and trying
service of nervous inactivity, listening by the
hour to the ripping of musketry up and down
the line, where whole corps are storming the
burning woods, breathing the drifting sulphurous smoke, and waiting, waiting.

No wonder the captain is nervous and irri-
table, and thankful for the setting sun and the
jaded orderly who brings him orders to be ready
to move at two o'clock in the morning. To the
left, always to the left. A vision of the imper-
turbable commander-in-chief rises from the
cramped lines within that yellow envelope. To
wait is patience ; to move is destiny.

The quartermaster, followed by his queer at-
tendant grinning from ear to ear, or rather up
toward one ear in particular, to see the boys at
the front, comes charging at a walk on the
ledge of rocks where the hungry officers are
seated.

"Just the man we want, Charley," cries

Lieutenant Sanderson, coming over to take the welcome coffee-pot. " Major Black has lost a collar-bone, and the doctor is looking for a substitute."

"Don't let him guy you, Charley," said Mink. " You've got the fresh bloom of the wagons on you. It does one good to see you rise out of these d—— hot weeds."

Charley is a privileged character at the front, and as he dismounts and leads his stumbling gray among the guns, the merriment goes with him, as the laughing wavelets follow the gliding boat.

" Dry up ! " " Come off ! " " Yous no good ! " are the burden of Charley's rejoinder. In an absent-minded way he is thinking of the Confederate prisoner hustled through these same guns, and of the other battery masked not so very far away. Kicking the stones and weeds, he wanders over to the thicket for a whip. He twists off a chestnut sprout, and tucks a spray of wild roses in old gray's headstall. At his feet is a cart rut leading into a tunnel of green. Charley wanders on into the cool retreat. There is the wall of stones beside the path. He sees before him the real counterpart of the picture the wounded Virginian painted on his brain in the shade of the hospital tree. Why not ride over

and send a message to that " pooty " Falmouth
girl? The boys think he is a fool. He has a
vague idea of distinguishing himself. He clam-
bers into the saddle, and rides down the path,
wagging his head and working his shoulders,
and doubtless thinking queer thoughts as his
horse picks his way among the outcropping
rocks.

" Halt! " cried a blue picket, rising out of
the bushes. " Where do you think you are
going, you blooming idiot? "

" I dun'no'," said Charley. "Do y-y-
you? "

" Yes ; you're going straight to the devil,"
said the man, laughing. " I fired my gun at
a sneaking rebel just now. Are you deaf?
Turn back, you fool; " and the man lazily
drew his ramrod to reload.

" Good-by," said Charley, making a hideous
face at the picket as he plied whip and heels to
his horse, and shot around a bend in the tunnel of green, chuckling and bumping like an
ape on horseback.

A quarter of a mile further on he is halted
again with a round oath, and a black rifle-bar-
rel levelled at his breast.

" You're my prisoner ; 'light off that
horse."

" Tha-tha-t's all right," said Charley, slid-
ing down to the ground as he was ordered.
" That's w'at I comed fur."

" You want to desert, do you, you lousy
Yankee ? You don't look like we-uns wanted
you."

" You're a l-l-liar," screamed Charley. " I
don't want to de-de-desert. I want ter see
Capt'n Chew. Didn't ye never see a flag o'
truce ? " said Charley, whipping a dirty cotton
handkerchief out of his pocket.

The Confederate picket called a comrade to
take his place, and started to the rear, leading
the horse and cursing and wondering by turns
at the curious fish he had taken in his net.

" You take me to Cap'n Chew's b-battery,"
said Charley, turning back on his guard, " 'cos
his brother is a-dyin' over yonder."

" You're a fool," said the guard, and turning up the hill to the right, he drove his charge
into a park of shining Napoleons crowning a
rocky ledge, with lunettes of rails and dirt
circling in front of each frowning gun.

" I've brought you a lunatic," said the
picket, addressing himself to the surging circle
of men and officers. " He has some sort of a
message for Captain Chew."

In his embarrassment, Charley more than

justified his keeper's description by grimaces and writhings.

" Be you Cap'n Bob Ch-Chew ? '' cried Charley, cutting a circle in the air with his thumb, and jabbing his head sideways at the officer he elected for the Captain.

" Yes," said the Captain ; " go on.''

" Well, then,'' began Charley, gathering himself together for a long speech, " your brother Lew sent me over here t' tell you t' tell that pooty gal in Fal-Fal-mouth that he got his arm shot, an' can't m-m-marry her next week.''

" Come to my tent," said the Captain, parting his way through the crowd and taking Charley by the arm.

There was a long interview between the two, in which Charley described as best he could the desperate situation of the young Virginian.

" He's got ter have his arm took off short,'' said Charley.

The excited brother walked up and down under the trees. " You are an artillery-man ? '' said the Captain, halting square in front of our hero.

" No ; n-nothin' but a sub-sta-sta-tute,'' said Charley.

" How did you get here ? '' said the other.

"I come up along o' the quartermaster to bring the Cap'n his coffee, an' I rid out here t' tell you how Lew was shot, an' couldn't m-m-marry the pooty gal," said Charley, with a great and successful effort.

"You belong to a battery?"

"Yes, I do."

"What one?"

"Battery k-k-Q."

"And who commands Battery Q?"

"Cap'n Ne-Neal."

"Where is Captain Neal's Battery Q?"

"No ma-ma-matter," said Charley, with a writhing contortion that winked one eye involuntarily. "I guess I told ye all I k-k-know."

"And I reckon you are a pretty good soldier, and don't know it," said Captain Chew. "I suppose you want to go back to Battery Q?"

"I knowed you'd s-send me back s-safe," said Charley, "'cos I cum for Lew."

The Captain had a consultation with his officers, during which the guard again took charge of the prisoner.

"Many more like you-uns 'mongst the Yanks?" said a long-geared driver, lifting Charley's cap from his head.

"You ain't n-no good," said Charley. "Gimme that cap."

" Look alive, boys ! " said the other ; " he's gettin' ready to jump down his throat."

" Gimme that cap ! " screamed Charley, making a futile effort to reach it from the long driver's hand.

The high words and jeering laughter reached the ears of Captain Bob Chew, who strode to Charley's side with flashing eyes. " This young gentleman is a friend of mine," said he, " and I will punish the first man who insults him by word or look. Smith, hand him his cap. Now say, ' I beg your pardon, sir.' Very well, sir. Now go back to your team. Now, my boy," said Captain Chew, " I am going to send you back, with a letter to your Captain, and with a bundle of clothing which I am sure you will deliver safely to my poor brother."

The gray horse, with his frying-pans and nose-bags, was led out, and the Confederate Captain held Charley's stirrup with all the politeness he would have shown a fine lady. The bundle of clothing was strapped fast behind his saddle. The directions for placing him outside the lines were carefully given to the officer of the pickets.

" And now, my fine fellow," said Captain Chew, grasping Charley's hand, " you have done me a service I am powerless to repay. Good-by, and God bless you ! And d—— the man that dares to do you harm ! "

By this time the soft moonlight was falling through the tree-tops. The little company of Charley's escort vied with each other to do him honor. They shook hands with him all round at the outpost, and gave the gray horse a friendly whack at parting.

It was nine o'clock, and the men of Battery Q were sleeping under the carriages, when an infantry picket emerged from the tunnel of green leading Charley's horse, that afflicted young gentleman sitting bolt-upright in the saddle, as proud as a knight.

Mink and Sanderson and Captain Neal were seated on the supper rocks in the moonlight, canvassing the disappearance of Charley. The two other lieutenants were already rolled up in their blankets.

On came the corporal of the guard conducting the picket, and riding between them the silent culprit. Captain Neal sprang to his feet.

" Where in thunder have you been, Charley? We never expected to see you alive."

" Oh, that's all r-right, Capt'n. I've been over to see the J-Johnnies. Here's a l-letter for you."

" Is he crazy? " muttered Captain Neal, as he took the letter to the light of a smouldering fire.

" Captain Neal, Battery Q. Politeness of Charley."

The letter conveyed the compliments of Captain Robert Chew to Captain Neal, stating in brief the service Charley had rendered, and begging the Captain to see that the bundle of clothing was delivered as directed.

In five minutes half the battery was awake and crowding around the hero of the adventure.

" These things must be delivered at once," said Captain Neal, in his short, nervous way. " The trains are marching. Charley will have to move with us to-night. Look here, Mink, can Charley ride your horse? "

" Of course," said Mink. " He can ride the devil, once put him in the saddle."

" Have him saddled, then," said the Captain, " and strap that bundle behind as taut as a sail in the wind. Order both buglers to saddle. Ho, Dick ! Where are you?. Put the saddle on Black Prince. We will execute this little commission in state," said the Captain, walking nervously back and forth on the turf. " And all honor to Charley ! "

The boys howled with delight.

When the horses came up, the two natty buglers sitting erect and silent, sniffing the fun like their mounts, Captain Neal turned to Charley :

" You are going to ride with me, young man. I expect you to stick to my off-stirrup like a chestnut burr to a sheep's wool. Do you understand ? "

" I understa-sta-stand," said Charley, " you bet."

The boys held the curb of Mink's mettlesome chestnut until stirrup and rein were adjusted to Charley's satisfaction ; then the Captain swung himself into the saddle.

Three cheers and a tiger were given for Charley Fitch as the snorting horses sprang forward over the turf. The Captain turned out of his way to leap a log or a ditch, but Charley, with his telescope cap clawed down to his lopping ears, was square with his elbow, never before and never behind ; and the silent buglers were plunging after them, keeping a mathematical interval, with their chins in the air, their elbows squared, and their brazen bugles flashing from the small of their backs. Over a ridge and down a bank they shoot, out on to the silent turnpike, white in the moon-

light, four sets of hoofs ringing on the hard
road-bed. To Charley it is the proudest moment of his life as he glances between the sharp
ears of the leaping chestnut, and then twists
his eyes and mouth on the glittering shoulder-
knots of the Captain.

"You ride like a brick," said the Captain,
drawing rein for the first time.

" The boys th-th-thought I was a fool," said
Charley.

" Tom Brown was shot to-day," said the
Captain. "Would you like his team?"

"Yes, Captain, I would. Will ye le-let
me?"

"If you think you could take a new uniform
and keep it clean."

"By gum!" cried Charley; "I'll be the
biggest dandy in the b-battery!"

" Then you shall have it, my boy," said the
Captain; "and here we go."

And away they tore in the yellow moonlight,
until they were close upon the moving lights
under the hospital tree. The silent buglers
took the panting horses. The Captain loosened
the bundle of clothing, and handed it to Charley.

The wretched company had increased its
circumference under the tree, but Charley

picked his unerring way among the wounded
until he reached the little circle of gray coats.

" Lew Chew ! " cried Charley.

" Here," said the young Virginian, raising
his sound arm, and looking out of the shadows
at the strange visitor and at the tall officer following.

" Here's the things yer b-brother sent," said
Charley, laying the bundle beside him. " I
told him you c-couldn't come to marry the
pooty gal."

"Have you seen my brother ? " cried the
happy boy. " God forgive me, I didn't understand you ! " And he was wringing Charley's
hand.

" Yes," said the Captain ; " he has been
through the lines. Heaven only knows how he
did it ! Here is the letter your brother wrote
me. Keep it while I go and see what can be
done for your comfort."

The poor wounded boy could hardly believe
he was awake ; it was all too good to be true.
During the Captain's prolonged absence, Charley dilated on the scenes and events of his passage across the lines, and his short sojourn in
the Confederate battery, with wonderful volu-
bility for him, and with involuntary gyrations
and convulsions and grimaces, which were by

no means the cause of the happy Virginian's half-hysterical glee. The wounded arm was not to be amputated.

"You are a brick," cried the Virginian, wringing Charley's hand for the twentieth time.

And then came the other brick, Captain Neal, with the chief surgeon in tow, and two muscular hospital nurses.

"We have no use for bridegrooms-elect," said the doctor. "Let's rob the government this time, and send him back by the same underground road." Then to the bearers, "Bring that man carefully out of the crowd."

"Now hold the lantern here." It is the Captain speaking. "Here is your parole ; sign it. We believe you will keep it like an honorable gentleman until you are notified of your official exchange ; and here is a letter to your brother."

The letter conveyed the compliments of Captain John Neal to Captain Robert Chew, and congratulations to the bride-elect.

The wounded prisoner was lifted into the saddle by Bugler Ohld, who walked at his side. He was sent down the tunnel of green on the worthless gray, and before marching-time in the morning, the old horse came back with Captain Chew's card nailed to the empty saddle.

For five days of merry fighting the rejuve-
nated Charley, in a brand-new uniform, sat his
lead-team blinking and grimacing at the fiery
shells dealing destruction about him. On the
sixth he presented himself before the Captain,
heels together and head up. Sitha Charley:
"It ain't m-my fault, Capt'n. I know I ain't
ornam-m-mental on a lead-team. Guess I better go back an' clean up old Spence. He ain't
no good the way he is."

The Horses that Responded

THE HORSES THAT RESPONDED

WHEN Lieutenants Mink and Sanderson of Battery Q felt the crying need of other society than that of their martial comrades of the mess, they ordered their horses and took their way to the red brick house on the hill, surrounded by tall locusts and elms shaped like umbrellas. There lived the old Colonel Nicholas Randolph, an invalided relic of earlier wars, and his two daughters, Trot and Plumb.

The way lay through a narrow lane, whose walls of stone were not available for fuel in the camps. The old house was within the lines, and for the protection of their new-found friends the two young officers had billeted a battery guard on the place.

The youngsters were always received by the old Colonel with a pompous oration. all just as if he had never seen them before.

"Will one of you gentlemen oblige an old wreck by opening that doah into the hallway? I thank you, sir. Ge—urls! Ge—urls!

"The old times have gone, sir. The Old Dominion is crushed for the time being, sir, under the heel of the invader. My honored friend, Bob Lee, will return to the fair fields of Culpepper County. In the meantime, while we are waiting fo' Bob as it were, the flowing bowl of the house of Randolph is at the service of the invader within its gates. If I could get off the small of my back, gentlemen, I should be riding with Bob and hunting such gallant game as you gentlemen I see befo' me, instead of grinning at you between two ornery old carpet slippers, the helpless old booby that I am."

The tall, fair daughters of Nicholas Randolph stand responsive, in the old doorway, to the summons of their father.

"Trot, my dear, and Plumb, you are not unacquainted with the cultured gentlemen from the North who have honored me with their company this evening."

It is one o'clock by the tall old timekeeper in the hall.

"Come here, Plumb, you huzzy, and shift my left foot the sixteenth of an inch to the right. Now bring a bottle of the '56 grape. If Nicholas Randolph, Esquire, is *hors de combat* for the time being, gentlemen, I reckon he can fire one more volley of grape into you fascinating gentlemen from the invading artillery.''

'' And there is not a thirsty beggar of us in Battery Q knows how to dodge that sort of ammunition,'' said Mink, stretching out his long legs, and toeing over to keep his spurs out of the ancient flowered carpet.

'' By the way, Colonel, I brought you a bundle of the latest New York papers.''

'' Burn New York ! '' cried the old man out of the depth of his cushions. '' Saving your presence, gentlemen, what irritates me is that that youngster [Mink is out in the gallery, despatching the guard to his saddle pockets], ova'-whelming us all with kindness, is a bohn gentleman from the guns on his cap to the spurs on his heels when he's no business to be, by gad, sir ! and I am a disgrace to Virginia, but I love you both, sir.''

The grizzled old Colonel, with his thin, high nose like a hawk's beak, and two restless gray eyes twinkling out of two cavernous sally-ports, the bony head fringed with a bristling abatis of coarse iron-gray hair, is literally resting on the small of his back. His feet are elevated on a padded support nearly as high as the back of his chair. His rheumatic hands, the purple fingers stiffened outward at an obtuse angle with the palms, lie restless at his sides. The Colonel rests in a nest of cushions, like a Coehorn mortar in its bed, and the whole complex outfit is mounted on wheels. The door-sills were levelled twenty years ago for the easy transit of the old master's gun-carriage, who thunders at his attendants on his way to the gallery as he stormed Chapultepec.

Mink, with the bundle of papers in his hand, whispered an order to the guard, and as the Colonel's car rolled through the doorway, that belted and shining soldier presented sabre. A moist light shone in the old man's eyes, and his right hand struggled with the cushions.

"By the left flank!" he cried. "March! Front!—Now, my dears, for the glasses."

"Let me name the toast," said Mink. "'To the days when we shall all be at peace.'" And it was turned off silently, pretty Trot touching her daddy's lips with the clumsy little one-legged cup of cut glass.

"With your consent, Colonel," said Mink, "Miss Plumb and I are going for another gallop out toward the mountain. I'll detail Sanderson to stay with you and hold Miss Randolph's yarn."

"No!" cried the Colonel. "Plumb shall

not go. The roads are not safe. I'll not have you captured in the company of my daughter, sir."

This rejoinder from the Colonel was no more than Mink expected, and the velvet - tongued Plumb hovered persuasive, as usual, over her daddy's chair until the old gentleman came round to her way of thinking.

"I've struck my colors," said the Colonel, "so many times to that girl already, I may as well haul down the garrison flag altogether and burn the staff—hey, Lieutenant?"

The soft air was loaded with the perfume of honeysuckles from the curtain of vines closing the south end of the high Doric porch. By turning his head to one side the Colonel looked out over his fenceless fields to the purple walls of the Blue Ridge. There was not a visible sign of the great army camping so near, except perhaps in the dearth of rails and stacks, and in the plenitude of crows and buzzards flapping against the cloudless sky. Down by the entrance gate two orderlies stood with the horses, and the Colonel asked that the animals be brought in on the drive, for, after all these years, his heart was still true to a horse.

The old man's appreciative eye ran over the powerful shoulders, short back, and flat legs of

Mink's chestnut, and then up to the animal's bony head and large, nervous nostril.

"There's a horse, sir," said the Colonel. "If you ever get in a tight place, Mr. Mink, big as you are, burn my body but he will carry you out of it."

"When he gets in a tight place," said Sanderson, "he rides a government horse. What do you think of my bay, Colonel? Swing him around, Dennis. Miss Plumb will ride him to-day."

"Plumb will have her hands full," muttered the Colonel, "but she can ride him, sir; if she couldn't, sir, I'd cut her off without a shilling. I raised my girls in the paddock with the colts;" and the Colonel fed his eyes complacently on the glossy coats of the horses, reflecting the blue of the sky above and catching the warm lights from below. "Take up another link in the curb chain," said the Colonel, as Mink walked over to inspect his orderly's work and give another strain to the girths of the young lady's saddle; "hey, Mr. Sanderson, you know his mouth."

And here comes Plumb as fresh as a peach, with a kiss for the Colonel, and one little hand for Lieutenant Sanderson, who has furnished her mount—Plumb in a ravishing habit of gray,

with a white felt hat on her chestnut hair,
which falls behind in a net, according to the
fashion of that benighted time, a red rose at
her throat, and a stiff little scarlet feather in her
hat-band, complimentary to the colors of her
artillery escort.

The pair—shall I say the lovers? I fear so ;
for that rogue of a Mink was quite equal to the
indiscretion, and young girls were never yet
proof against the wiles of the enemy—rode
demurely down the pied avenue. Then, too,
when Mink whistled up his orderly and graciously excused his further attendance, that
shrewd young fellow concluded it was a far
gone case, and chuckled and winked to himself
as he galloped across the fields to the camp.

It is of no great moment to anyone but
themselves just what these young persons said to
each other as they rode at a walk under the
spreading trees, their quiet horses treading the
lacework of sunshine and shadow that dappled
the road. But the way in which they said it,
the bending forward with appealing gesture of
one, and the averted head of the other, the
movement of the shoulders, the touch of hands,
the quiet laughter, the steady gaze of four eyes
firing double-barrelled volleys at each other !

Love - making on horseback is much more

dignified and reserved than the same youthful pursuit in a carriage. It leaves more to be hoped for and less to be regretted.

It is not all walking in the shade, for the fresh horses now and then gallop on in the sunlight, and the mountains are rising and coming to meet them. It is not a safe country for an officer of the Army of the Potomac to be riding in, but Lieutenant Mink and Miss Plumb in her gray habit have forgotten everything but each other. Ten miles have they ridden into the jaws of danger, serenely oblivious of the Colonel's parting injunction.

Lieutenant Mink alighted, alarmed at length by their very nearness to the mountains, and, looking nervously about him, tightened the girths of the saddles. A mile back they had met a sober-looking old farmer bestride a steady-going horse, and they had been too absorbed to notice that he had soon thereafter quickened his pace, looking back as he rode.

Mink kept his counsel as they galloped rapidly on the return, thinking to spare his companion unnecessary anxiety, but pretty Plumb knew more of the resorts of the partisan rangers than he. As the sun sank at their backs, throwing longer shadows before, that prudent young lady thought it her duty to speak.

"I have heard," said Mink, laughing, and carelessly snipping his boot with his whip, "that it is the part of good generalship to be always prepared for surprise ; to have one's army in hand, you know. Now I am the general to-day, and you are the army. The first lesson for the army to learn is blind obedience. You are a soldier's daughter, my dear Miss Plumb——"

"And half a soldier myself," said she, looking admiringly at her broad-shouldered escort. "I think I should love a charge."

"You may have it, my dear," said Mink. "In any event it is no surrender." And then turning a grave, penetrating look on his pretty companion : "You are sure you will obey the word of command, whatever it is, and that instantly?"

"Whatever it is, and instantly," said she, looking up into the eyes of her general.

"Even if I ride one way and order you another ?"

"Even so, I will obey."

A half mile in front, five men, well mounted and well armed, and accompanied by the old farmer bestride the steady-going horse, himself now carrying a gun, are riding in pursuit of the reckless officer and the lady. The shoe-prints are clearly impressed in the sand, for the old farmer had guided his horse to one side, not to disturb the trail.

" You said the officer and the lady was ridin' a fine pair o' horses, Uncle Billy," said the leader of the band.

" Jes so, Cap' ; an' you'll bar me out when ye see them hosses. Nothin' finer haint gone over these roads lately."

" Mighty sorry, gentlemen, to make the gal walk and rob her of her cavalier too. But I reckon there are three animals in that outfit we all will have to take charge of. When they come in sight, you Jack, and you Tom, just ride out on the flanks. I expect they'll give up easy."

The raiders had drawn rein at the foot of a hill, and at this stage of the conversation were a hundred yards from the top, well bunched in the road, and proceeding at a walk. At the same moment Lieutenant Mink, who was half a length ahead of Miss Plumb, intent on getting the first glance over the hill, handed his whip to his companion.

" Now, my dear, for that charge," he said, drawing his sabre from its lashings under the skirts of his saddle. " Ride close to my side and ride hard."

Then shooting on to the top of the hill, with a touch of his heel that stung the nerves of the

chestnut and tautened the reins like a bow-string,
Mink swung the glittering blade above his head
and shouted with all his lungs, "Here they are,
boys! Charge!"

In that instant the bay sprang to his side,
little Plumb's teeth set and her eyes flashing
with excitement. Down the hill the gallant
animals plunged to the charge, with a furious
momentum that Mink well knew would be irresistible at so short a dash. The bunch of
horsemen parted each way, perceiving it was to
be a chase instead of a halt. But Lieutenant
Mink was not content even with this advantage,
and, seeing the Captain of the rangers cocking
his rifle, swerved the big chestnut to the left,
and, as he shot by, swung his long arm around
the Captain's neck and dropped him over his
horse's crupper into the road, as if the man had
been a sack of grain.

And on the powerful, mettlesome horses
plunged, now spurning the level road under
their ringing hoofs, their riders feeling their
superb muscles working under them like the
throb of an engine. A quarter of a mile is
gained at the start and not a word has been
spoken, although Mink has turned a satisfied
eye on plucky little Plumb flying at his side,
with her white teeth set hard and tears of ex-

citement glistening in her eyes. Four bullets
have indeed whistled high over their charmed
heads, and he draws a breath of relief for the
sake of his companion in peril. Then Mink
drops his sabre into its scabbard, and leans forward to take a good look in Miss Plumb's face;
their hands meet, and he laughs merrily to re-
assure her, and she laughs a little hysterically
in return.

"My darling, you are a worthy daughter of
the old Colonel, and I am proud of you. One
—two—three—four—did you happen to hear
the Captain's gun?" said Mink. "I fancy he's
not in the race. Ease 'em up, my dear," he
continued; "there is time enough to run when
we are pressed."

But the horses refused to be eased, and the
chestnut took much coaxing before he could be
persuaded to slacken his pace.

There was a scattering pursuit, but it was
hopeless from the first, for the nervous, high-
strung horses of the pursued party sprang forward at the slightest slackening of the rein, running with a joyous, high-headed abandon that
kept them easily out of range.

The Colonel and his party were still on the
gallery when the wanderers rode up the drive,
their mounts as wet as if they had just swum

the river, and altogether in finer form than when they walked out of the gate.

Little Plumb was as cool as a veteran, not a fold of her habit disarranged, and after kissing her father she gave him the humorous side of the charge and the fate of the burly Captain.

" Shiver my trunnions ! " cried the Colonel, glaring first at his daughter and then at Lieuten- ant Mink, leaning with his hands in his pock- ets against a Doric pillar, and then over the rail at the two quiet horses walking off in charge of the orderlies, " dash my buttons, if I know which of the four I admire most ! "

" Lights Out ! 'Liz'beth Rachael "

A MONOLOGUE

"LIGHTS OUT! 'LIZ'BETH RACHAEL."

IT was all on account o' 'Liz'beth Rachael.

I don't look like a man as would break his heart over a woman, do I? I ax you, comrades, an' I ax you square, ef I look like I had too much sentiment into my make - up? I'm sort o' plain, humspun ole Chris' Bradley, I be; an' that's what everybody knows me fur aroun' here. Post nights and camp - fires an' meetin' a Sunday is all the dissipation I takes to—'cept when the chores is done on the farm a-nights I puts on my G.A.R. hat, an' mebby my vest, an' goes up to the village to see the boys.

You didn't jest know 'Liz'beth Rachael, you two, an' you come a long ways to 'tend the buryin', an' I'm partic'lar obleeged to the heft o' Snyder Post as come along with ye. I kallate we sha'n't never see the boys fire a volley over a woman's grave agin.

Poor 'Liz'beth Rachael! She'd a' been

proud to heard the guns. An' jest afore we
left the buryin'-ground, when it was growin'
sort o' meller an' dusky, an' drefful still after
the volley, an' the powder-smoke was hangin'
to the bushes, an' all the boys was lookin' inter
their hats, to see old Bugler Frisbee step out
on the hillside, so straight an' dark agin the
yeller sky, an' blow them powerful tender
notes that goes rite through a soldier's heart—
" Lights out ! 'Liz'beth Rachael—Lights out !
'Liz'beth Rachael—L-i-g-h-t-s o-u-t ! "

I ain't much onto poetry, comrades, but
that air business tuk a powerful hold on my
feelin's. Seein' all them gray heads bowed
under the old flag-staff, an' it hevin' scarcely
enough rags left onto it to flutter in the wind,
an' the smell o' the powder agin, jest took me
plum back to the day when Dick Welton fell
dead under that same flag-staff, an' Jones an'
Color-Sergeant Brown afore him, in less time
than it takes to tell ye. Dick was 'Liz'beth
Rachael's man, ye understand.

Like to hear the story, would ye? Well,
comrades, I 'low I feel more like marchin'
over the old ground again to-night than ever I
did afore. Things is freshened up in my mind,
like. I'm a boy agin, doin' odd chores round
the village, carryin' bundles in the harvest field

an' pickin' thistles out o' my toes an' nussin'
stone-bruises on my heels, an' gettin' a little
schoolin' in the winter, an' fightin' the other
boys on account o' 'Liz'beth Rachael.

I was alus at the foot o' the class an' 'Liz'-
beth Rachael alus up to the head, fur she was
quick to learn, an' that's the reason I hated
the school—fur keepin' us so fur apart. Outside we jest growed up together, an' nobody
interfered, an' everybody tuk it all fur granted,
same as I did, an' same for 'Liz'beth Rachael.

There was jest one thing come betwixt us
two to spile the dress-parade, an' I don't 'low
to favor myself, comrades—not partic'lar on
the night o' 'Liz'beth Rachael's buryin'.
When things worried me, an' likewise when I
had too much luck, I liquored accordin', an'
that set all the women advisin' 'Liz'beth Rachael, an' 'Liz'beth Rachael advisin' me. She
was mighty sweet an' pooty them days — tall
an' trim as a sergeant - major, an' sassy as a
lieutenant home on leave, an' when she told
me off fur punishment duty I tuk the discipline
some quieter than ever I did in the field.

But 'twa'n't no use. Much as I wanted to
do right an'. please 'Liz'beth Rachael—an' I
loved her more'n all the world beside—somethin' would turn up to put me back in the

police squad, an' then, bless her, she'd take
me out o' the guard-house an' we'd be somethin' more'n comrades agin, goin' to meetin'
together—'Liz'beth Rachael sung in the choir
—an' plannin' to take the old folks' farm on
shares, an' reformin', an' all that.

I 'lowed to do right, comrades, but makin'
promises to 'Liz'beth Rachael was like startin'
on a charge, double-quickin', an' cheerin' an'
howlin' to keep your courage up until, suddin-
like, somethin' happens to change yer mind.
You meet up with somethin' you didn't expect. I didn't have the pluck to hug the
ground an' scrape up a bit o' cover—alus found
myself in full retreat afore I knowed it.

Along then the old folks turned agin me,
an' Dick Welton took to drivin' over from the
Cross Roads, an 'Liz'beth Rachael sort o'
favored him —some folks said to make me
jealous, but I couldn't believe that o' 'Liz'beth
Rachael — an' I lost heart an' jest clean deserted to the enemy.

That spring the war broke out, an' Dick
jumped in and raised the first company in the
county, an' everybody swore by Dick, an'
'Liz'beth Rachael couldn't a' helped lovin'
him ef she'd tried. Pretty much all the gals in
the village did the same, an' I didn't blame 'em.

'Liz'beth Rachael cried an' tuk on an' said she'd alus be my friend, an' made me promise to reform for her sake.

Jest before the company started they was fast married in the church, an' I went up with the rest an' saw it all through, jest as if I didn't care. I tell you it didn't take me long to find out that Pumford wa'n't no place for me to stop in, an' I turned out an' 'listed in Dick's company afore it left the State.

Somehow I couldn't never keep it in my mind that Dick was my rival an' actually the husband of 'Liz'beth Rachael—he was so brave an' keerful o' the boys, he seemed more like a big brother. He was some older'n me.

You was both of ye at Antietam !

Well, now, shake.

What — up on the right, too ? Hooray ! Shake again. You'll understand it all. That's where we left poor Dick in the smoke that September Sunday.

You remember how we got onto the skirmish line in the dusk, an' how the line run across the field in the open an' then into the woods on the flank, an' the brush we had with the Johnnies afore we settled down an' got quiet in the dark ?

Shake !

An' how the last scatterin' shots went bang-
bang in the pastur', an' boom - boom in the
woods, an' sparkled like fire-flies in the grass ?
Shake !

An' then how mortal still it got, an' cold,
an' the shuckin' o' the gun-wheels up on the
ridge behind whar the batteries was unlimber-
in' an' gettin' quiet into place ; an' the chop-
pin' an' poundin' of the Johnnies buildin' up
the granite ledges into breastworks, an' the
sound of ammunition-wagons all night on the
road by the Dunker Church.
Shake ! shake ! We was there !

Dear me ! I can smell the pastur', wet with
the dew, an' see the stars shinin' above the
woods to the right—so cold and far off, as if
'twa'n't none o' their fight.

Creepy, now wa'n't it, boys, layin' thar lis-
tenin' to the preparations — wonderin' whar
ye'd be same time next night—battery fellers
stumblin' on ye in the dark huntin' for water
to fill the sponge-buckets, an' we a-knowin'
the ball would open the minute it got light
enough to see the gray devils layin' out in front ?

But I'm forgettin' all about Captain Dick.

It was helter-skelter afore noon over in front
of that little chapel. We got orders to charge
on a brigade formin' to strike our flank, an'

we charged pell-mell down the slope, the big
guns up above roarin' over our heads and
plungin' shell into the woods an' the church.
The brigade we started for slumped off to the
right an' lapped in behind us an' got scooped
up by the troops follerin', an' all the time we
was pushin' back the Johnnies in front, rallyin'
up with the colors — blazin' right an' left —
smoke too thick to breathe easy—shells bustin'
everywhere—flag down—flag up—boys didn't
know when they was hit — captains gettin'
scarce — Color - Sergeant Brown lyin' dead
across that same old stick you seen to - day
with the rags onto it.

Cap'n Dick rolled him off an' raised the
colors once more, an' we all yelled an' cheered,
an' some jest cried with excitement but banged
away all the same, an' more loaded and fired
still as mice ; an' sudden like all the rebs
melted away in front of us into the ground, an'
we set up a cheer an' went ahead after Captain
Dick, the staff in one hand an' holdin' up the
colors on the pint of his sword with the other,
an', my God ! the ground afore us jest blazed
with a sheet o' fire from behind a step-off o'
granite rock as nobody could see, an' Captain
Dick went down an' half the boys along with
him.   Poor old Dick knowed he was done for,

237

an' he throwed the flag back with all his strength, an' we carried it away over the boys lyin' wounded an' dead on the pastur',—an' I thought o' 'Liz'beth Rachael waitin' home an' her Dick trampled among the nameless dead. An' that's how we cum to call the post after Dick—"Richard Welton Post, G.A.R., No. 140."

When we got a stray letter from home there was always some bad news about 'Liz'beth Rachael. There was plenty of home folks here in Pumford lost kin that day—half the women was dressed in black—but none of 'em took it so hard as 'Liz'beth Rachael. First she was reg'lar sick with grief an' worrit, an' then the baby died, an' she was clean gone out of her head. For weeks and months she lay sick with fever, an' the neighbors never expected her to get well. An' when she did cum round she couldn't seem to remember anything 'cept Dick an' the war an' the baby that was dead.

It's thirty years now since we all come home —seems like yesterday—ragged an' dirty uniforms—only twenty in the company—old flag some torn an' shot up, but ye could read the names o' battles in gold letters on every stripe, white an' red — jest thirteen of 'em. We marched over from the railroad in the dust an' sun—ten miles—route step, heads up. Women to the gates with lemonade an' cake—harvest hands on the fences, villages turnin' out. Men an' boys follerin' a - foot, a - horseback, an' in wagins.

All Pumford was on the Mill hill to meet us, an' they fell on us ten to one.

You bet, comrades, I was lookin' for 'Liz-'beth Rachael's 'mongst the faces, an' thar it was, the eagerest, wildest - eyed ye ever seen, chargin' clean through the ranks afore all the rest, an' when she didn't find Dick she begun to call him out loud an' run among us an' stare at each of us with her wild, dry eyes. She didn't even know me — 'Liz'beth Rachael didn't. So we jest told her that Dick hadn't got along yet, an' then Fred Gibbs an' me led her away to some o' the women in black clothes that was cryin' together behind the rest, an' Mis' Wiggins, whose two boys was both killed, put her arms around 'Liz'beth Rachael an' comforted her the best she could.

It was dreadful hard lines, holdin' onto that little hand an' supportin' 'Liz'beth Rachael along, an' she not knowin' me, as growed up along with her an' loved her so long. Somehow the women was all a blur when we give her up to 'em, an' I pinted back to the boys.

Well, 'Liz'beth Rachael was jest the same
from that day on—always expectin' Dick, an'
always askin' fur him ef she met up with a soldier. She knowed all of us fur friends o'
Dick's when we had our rigimentals on, but
she never seemed to know one of us from
t'other. It was heart-breakin' to hear her ask
the same old question, " Whar's my Dick? "
an' bimeby we got to answer her, " Oh, he's
all right," an' that seemed to satisfy her, an'
everybody in the village come to answer her in
the same way, down to the little kids jest larn-
in' to talk.

When we organized the post we called it the
" Richard Welton Post, G.A.R., No. 140."
'Liz'beth Rachael seemed to think she had
some interest into it. Every other Friday
night she stood outside the door an' asked the
guard whar her Dick was, an' some o' the comrades brought their wives along reg'lar, jest to
talk to 'Liz'beth Rachael and take her home.
But 'twa'n't no use tryin' to keep her out of
Richard Welton Post when she 'lowed she belonged there, an' we talked the matter over,
an' all the comrades agreed that 'Liz'beth
Rachael couldn't do no harm if she was let to
set inside.

Now, that's the way her relations with the

post begun. After a while we made her a seat beside the chaplain, an' 'Liz'beth Rachael was always in it, and never knowed the pass-word nor yit the grip. We told her the word was " Dick," an' she comes up to the guard an' whispers " My Dick," an' he lets her by, an' she marches up an' salutes the commander jest like the rest, an' turns off to her reg'lar place. Little changes for her sake crep' in, one after another, an' ever since Major Wise's time, years ago, after the opening prayer the commander would stand up and strike his gavel an' look at 'Liz'beth Rachael, an' she would stand up an' say, " Where's my Dick ? " an' all the post would rise an' say, " Oh, he's all right," an' then go on with business jest as if she wa'n't there ; an' 'Liz'beth Rachael looked so contented an' happy, an' set so still, that we all felt glad to do so much for Dick's widow. And every post night, when the exercises was over, 'Liz'beth Rachael saluted and walked straight home, never lookin' to the right nor left, an' the armed guard was marchin' twenty paces behind her.

But I tell you, comrades, Decoration Day was the beginnin' an' end of the year for 'Liz'-beth Rachael. She had some sort of an idea that Dick had somethin' to do with the flag, an' nothin' would do but she must carry the old colors, an' carry them she did, as long as she lived, her thin gray hair uncovered to the sun an' the wind. Some of the women talked to her about Dick an' the baby until she kind o' got the two confounded, an' so, when we heaped the flowers on the little grave an' told her they was for Dick, she was so happy arrangin' the little flags an' wreaths on the green mound an' over the white headstone that she clean forgot to ask the old question.

Then, 'Liz'beth Rachael growed the heft of the flowers herself. That was her little cottage what we took her out from, with the rose-bushes trailin' over the shed an' the pinks an' pinys growin' in the garden an' the phlox an' 'zalias hidin' the fences. What with the locust-trees in bloom, an' the clover patch blowed out, it was sweet enough around whar 'Liz'beth Rachael lived to make a bumble-bee stagger.

Did ye take notice of the sign over the porch —it was half hid with climbin' roses to-day— " Richard Welton Post, G.A.R., No. 140," in red letters on a white board with a blue border ? Well, we had that lettered an' put up for her, an' she was as proud of it as a paintin'.

'Arly in the spring we ploughed the garden

an' dug the beds for her, an' sowed the seeds
an' did the pottin'-out—fur all winter 'Liz'-
beth Rachael had the windows an' the glass
shed full o' roses an' geraniums an' sich, an'
she never forgot to water an' tend um, nuther.
In the summer she might sell a nosegay to the
city folks, but afore the thirtieth day o' May
nobody couldn't buy a sprig.

One day Miss King—her folks come up from
Cincinnaty in the summer time — druv with
some strangers to see 'Liz'beth Rachael, an'
when they kem down to the gate, the'r arms
full o' roses, 'Liz'beth Rachael seen the flunky,
all buttons, standin' by the kerridge door, an'
she ups an' asks him, " Whar's my Dick ? "
an' the feller stared like he was shot, an' Miss
King took her hand in hern, with the tears in
her eyes, an' says, so sweet, " Oh, he's all
right."

Now, wa'n't that clever ? Everybody was
that a-way to 'Liz'beth Rachael.

A little afore she died her memory come
back to her like second sight. The women an'
the preacher told her about everything, an' she
thanked everybody for all what they had done
for her. She sent for me an' made me tell her
everything I could remember about Dick, an'
how he bore up the flag, an' all that happened

that day. An' I had to tell it to her over an'
over again, an' mebby if I disremembered some
little thing she'd pull me up an' say, " Chris,
you forgot about the shells burstin' overhead,"
or " You didn't tell me about the gun-wheels
soundin' in the night, just as Dick an' you
heard 'em," an' then I had to go over it all
again.

An' she talked to me about the old days before the war, an' remembered everything jest
as I remembered it. But never mind, comrades, about that part, 'Liz'beth Rachael is
gone, an' there'll be another vacant chair in
Richard Welton Post, G.A.R., No. 140, an'
when some old fire dog turns up in Pumford
with a cord on his hat or brass buttons on his
vest, as they mostly does, thar won't be no
'Liz'beth Rachael to ax him, " Whar's my
Dick ? "

The Widow of the General

THE WIDOW OF THE GENERAL

I N the quiet burial-ground of a little village by the sea, somewhere within the boundaries of the northern half of the restored Union, lie at rest two officers of the old army whom a difference of opinion — the one a native of Maine, and the other of Louisiana—for a time made enemies, but who now, reunited, are sleeping shoulder to shoulder in the last long sleep.

Once a year the two mounds are strewn, the one with roses, and the other with flowers of the magnolia and orange, and, strange to relate, the Southern blossoms are laid on the grave of the Northern soldier, while the flowers of the North are always heaped on the other mound.

A plain marble shaft rises above the head of the Northern soldier, white among the brown head - stones of six generations of sailors and fishermen.

On the principal face of the monument is the following inscription :

BRIG : GENERAL ——,
18—.   18—.
Dulce et decorum est pro patria mori.

And on the right-hand face, in incised letters of a much more recent date:

COLONEL ——,
Friend and Classmate.
Comrade.

In the same village by the sea lives a beautiful lady, the widow of the General. Although her hair has grown silvery gray with advancing years, time has dealt over gently with the pale thoughtful face and with the erect slender figure. All the year she wears the weeds and bands of widowhood, except on one particular day, and that the 30th of May, when it pleases this lady to go abroad radiant in a dainty costume of harmonious colors, which comes fresh from the modiste's on the evening before, and which is sent away on the day after to be sold in the city for the benefit of some charity. It is because, she says, weeds and flowers have no place together that she decks herself like a bride on this festival of the flowers, and goes forth to rejoice, leaving the shadow of her mourning behind.

In all her native village no young girl is more cheerful and contented with her lot than this lady in sombre black and spotless white, whose mind and fingers are busy all the days with projects of charity and dainty creations in needlework.

On winter nights, when storms are abroad, and the seas beat on the sands with a boom and roar like distant artillery, the General's widow sits closer to the fire, thankful that there is no war in the land, and if her thoughts wander away to the clash and tumult of other fields long since quiet, is it any wonder?

On a certain evening, when this lady's windows are open to the soft breath of spring, and when her eleventh dainty costume (she trusts it *is* dainty, although she has no heart to look at it) lies unopened in its box on the table, her thoughts have wandered still further away, to one of the frontier posts of the old army—a lieutenant's wife absorbed in all that took place between the rising of the sun and the going down of the garrison flag. She thought of many things, but most of a certain hare-brained lieutenant, who was forever getting her Jack into hot water on the strength of their having been classmates and roommates at the Academy; and how he got himself in hot water through his violent love for a girl from New York who descended on the garrison in the regular way, and how she coolly left him in ice-water when it came to a serious consideration of the differ-

ence between a silver leaf and a single bar.
She remembered that she herself had banished
him to bachelor quarters when she appeared at
the post, where she found the two lieutenants
living together, and quarrelling like monkeys
and parrots to make up for the prolonged inactivity of their regiment.

Once, during a little discussion as to rank,
Bob had sneered at Jack's three days' seniority,
and sworn hotly that he should be sorry to be
buried on the same field, except for the chance
—with his best bow—of Emily turning up with
more tears than she cared to waste on him.

And once, just before his resignation from
the old regiment to take up arms against us all,
Bob had said: "Take notice, Jack, I have
always wanted to quarrel with you, and never
had much success. Looks like my wildest
hopes would be more than gratified—ha, old
man?" And so they had hectored and nagged
and loved each other.

Bob had been living abroad since the close
of the war, broken in health and temper, but
now and then he wrote the most pathetic and
amusing letters to the widow of his old friend.

The widow of the General came back with
a start from the frontier post, listened for a
moment to the murmur of the surf, like *very*

distant artillery, and took from the table the last letter of this much-disappointed old soldier :

"MY DEAR MADAM AND FRIEND,—It is no matter where I am, but wheresoever that may be, I take the liberty to pray for your happiness as often as I venture to ask any official favors for myself. This morning—fact—I ran against Blowser, of the old regiment, steering a red mountain of flesh and a drove of little hillocks into a railway compartment too contracted for the old girl herself. The little fool pretended he didn't know me, and I shook him by the collar until he was as red as a lobster ; and then, says I, ' Blowser, I'll forgive you for the sake of your family,' and shoved him into the sardine-box. He enchanted me with American manners to that extent that I resolved to come home at once, and I have already taken passage in a sailing vessel, where I shall not be badgered ten times a day to bet my last stiver on the run of the ship. If you are all as polite as Blowser, I shall pack up my wooden leg and come back on the fastest steamer afloat.

" Otherwise I shall kiss the hand of my old friend in the early summer, and billet myself in quarters near by, where I can hobble over and hear all there is to be told about the man whom it has been my lot to love above all others. . . .

"Life has turned out for me very different from what I pictured it as a saphead subaltern ; but I want you to understand that I have nothing to regret except the misfortune of my birth on the wrong side of a family quarrel. Given the same problem again, I should solve it by the same suicidal folly. I am not a man without a country, for I can walk heartily under the old flag—and more—all I have to complain of is that I can't serve under it. During my best years I have been a man disbarred from the ranks of the profession he loved, and all for an accident of birth. I had no heart to enter a foreign army and cut throats for a beggarly salary.

"As for my old friend Jack, he might—he *should*—have lived on, an ornament to his profession and a comfort to his incomparable wife. I, on the contrary, should have died in the front of the battle, riddled, pulverized, as the only rational way out of the difficulty."

Here the General's widow shed a few tears, and folded the letter without re-reading further.

The village had been astir since early morn-

ing with the tramp of men and the sound of
drums and the laughter of children. The veterans, in their post uniforms, had marched and
countermarched on the broad grassy street,
carrying aloft their ragged flags, and all the
people cheering. At sunrise the old church-
yard had been heaped and strewn with fresh
flowers, and little printed cotton flags had been
thrust into each mound marking a soldier's
grave.

The General's widow, together with other
women similarly bereaved, but gayer and more
joyous in her spring attire than any of the
others, whether maids or mothers, has helped
the old soldiers in their beautiful work, strip-
ping her garden and grounds of flowers, until
to-morrow they will be as sombre and devoid
of color as herself. But, like *la cigale*, she
thinks only of to-day, glad in the warm sunshine and the cool east wind from the sea, and
glowing with gratitude to the soldiers and the
children who have jostled each other to lay
their tributes on the mound that covers her
General.

How joyous the world is, and how sweet and
fitting to live in it, hallowed by the memory of
her dead !

For four days the prevailing winds have

been from the east, cooling and refreshing to
the villagers and the workmen in the fields,
and inclining to drowsiness the dwellers in the
newly opened cottages. Day by day waves
have lapped gently on the beach, so that the
weakest bathers have scorned the ropes, and
the surfman has tied up to the buoy and gone
to sleep in his rocking boat. But all the time
the spreading waves from a great storm at sea,
hundreds of miles away, pushed along by the
unvarying winds, have been moving on the
unsuspecting coast, bringing nearer and nearer
that wonderful phenomenon of a raging sea
under a smiling summer sky.

Absorbed in the exercises of the morning,
the people have paid little heed to the roaring
of the surf, which has been rising steadily during the night. And now as they are dispersing
to their homes, news comes of the boisterous
behavior of the sea, and the curious begin to
move leisurely in the direction of the beach.
Arrived beyond the orchards, where one gets
the first glimpse of the ocean, there comes suddenly into view a great flashing wall of foam,
tumbling over and over on the reaches of beach
visible between the sand hills, and throwing
masses of spray above the tops of the highest
dunes, whereon the people are already gathering

in interested groups. Then the men and boys begin to run as if there were danger of the monster ceasing to rage, and all the fields are sprinkled with the people coming, and the hills are black with the people come, standing awe-struck among the tall grasses and the ragged plum-bushes.

On come the green ridges of water, one above another, each a huge curving wall break-ing with a deafening boom into a boiling, de-vouring mass of foam, coming on over the highest line of the beach, licking up tons of sand as it comes, and depositing it again as it surges into tameness against the foot of the an-cient dunes, and turns down within the beach a green foam - flecked current floating every-thing movable within its reach.

How the bath-men are hurrying to and fro roping the smaller houses to the larger ones, and how the captives at the ends of their tethers bob in the current like apples in a bowl of water! The boats are already haled into safety behind the hills.

Deeper and heavier grows the volume of water moving like a broad river between the crest of the beach and the foot of the sand hills, bearing brush and drift-wood and camp-chairs and occasionally a bath - house on its seething current, until, at the weakest point, the beach yields, and the flood pours back into the sea through a gorge cut in a moment, carrying out logs, houses, and chairs, to reappear like straws in the tumbling foam — to land for an instant on the wet sand, and then to be sucked back into the hungry waters.

The lady of the General is there, her festal robes fluttering and dampening in the sticky salt wind, and the veterans, in their shirt sleeves and hats bound round with gold cord, are running to and fro shouting in great glee, and rescuing whatever comes within their reach as if they were scouring over a conquered field —charging into the edge of the flood, and laying down plans to rescue groups of youngsters who have been surrounded unwittingly, as industriously as if they were at the pontoon-bridges again.

" The ball's open ! "

" Don't ye hear the rebel yell ? "

" Lay down quick ! there comes a shell ! "

" Nigger eat sponge cake ! "

How the old boys enjoy their holiday, and riot in the war of the elements !

Some tire of the spectacle, and go away, but others come to fill their places. Hour after hour the sea becomes more furious, the wind snipping off the crests of the waves until no eye can penetrate the thickening spray and spume. Out of the invisible the great walls of green chase each other, more majestic and irresistible than ever, and all the time the sky overhead is without a cloud, and behind, the heat is throbbing above the orchards and the village as if the land took no note of the sea.

The beach has risen foot after foot, built up by the layers of sand brought in and released by the boiling surf, until the bath - houses, which have clung to their foundations, look like hen-coops, with the flood swirling into the narrow strips of darkness under the eaves which were once the tops of doorways, and the shelters of oak boughs, built to protect the horses from the sun, are torn and dripping a few inches above the surface of the new beach.

Fascinated by the grandeur of the spectacle, and absorbed in watching the physical changes wrought in the land by this battle between the sand and the sea, the people linger on the dunes until sunset, and then hurry to their homes to snatch a mouthful of refreshment, and come again with thick wraps to crouch on the dry hills and watch and marvel.

The old soldiers have built fires of drift-wood behind the scarps of the sand hills, and as the widow of their beloved General comes again, they insist upon stationing her party at the camp fires while they go and come on the ridge to bring her news of the enemy.

Hark! what is that sound, half heard and half feared, which seems to come out of the darkness through the roaring of the surf? Not faint, as betokening distance, but undeterminable in the tumult of sound. Once!—doubted —the people murmur, " Did you hear ? " *Twice !* — feared — the crowd is hushed. *Thrice ! Thrice !* Then the people know they have heard guns from a crew in distress close behind the impassable wall—know that they are fellow-creatures facing death, actually but a few hundred yards off the beach, while practically they may be as many leagues away.

Boats are not to be thought of. The crew has come up from the station, and the old sol-diers are running to and fro with ropes, and help-ing to drag the mortar on to the highest sand hill. From time to time the guns are heard again—one—two—three, and rockets are sent up from the land, ploughing away into the gloom, and bursting over the breakers into flower-pots.

An hour has passed. The crews have come up from four miles to the north and from four miles to the south.

And now the eastern sky is reddening behind
the spume of the surf which hides the rising
moon. Again the guns—one—two—three—
and guided by the sound the practised eyes of
the surf-men, aided by the growing light, de-
tect a blotch of shadow through the veil of
spume that may be the spars of the wreck.

One after another the mortars throw their
shells athwart the sea, until at last a line is
found to be taut, and communication is established with something living on the ship.

In all the turmoil and excitement no one is
so calm and collected as the General's widow.
Who else, indeed, shall establish the hospital by
the fires in the lee of the sand dunes? Who
but her old soldiers shall be the stretcher-
bearers, and who but they her willing orderlies
eager to do her bidding—running post to the
village for blankets and stimulants, marshalling
the doctors, confiscating the available supplies
of the life - saving station, and ready to turn
carts and phaetons into ambulances, every old
boy a provost marshal in himself, sworn into
the service of the tall quiet lady wearing the
black ulster over the dainty spring costume?

The incomparable lady of the General, pupil
of the revered master who still lies alone on the
hill, putting into practice the old lessons of the

camp, decorating his memory with the substance of brave deeds, as she has just strewn his grave with the symbol of flowers.

The battle is over. The dead and the wounded are coming rapidly into the field hospital, tenderly borne by the practised old stretcher - bearers. A few have come ashore safely by the running rigging over the rope; but alas! more have been thrown up by the surf, beaten and mangled by the timbers of the breaking ship.

In the light of the flaring fires the unconscious, the dying, and the dead are gathered on the sand, the nurses and doctors busy with their ministrations. The tall lady of the General, mistress of every detail, is moving gently from group to group through the smoke, calling each of her veteran assistants by name, while the remnant of her old soldiers is posted in an impassable cordon to keep back the idle crowd of lookers-on.

One after another, with incredible labor, the half-drowned have been revived, broken limbs have been set, and the unhappy victims borne away through the summer night to comfortable quarters in the village.

Bodies are yet to be recovered from the waves, but only bodies. The gray banner of the coming day is already streaming above the pitiless sea, paling the light of the fires, and rendering more ghastly the scenes behind the sheltering dunes. The lady of the General shows no signs of fatigue and no abatement of energy, as constant to her self-imposed duty as her old guard, silhouetted damp and chilly against the morning.

Besides the hopelessly dead, covered tenderly from sight, there is but one remaining tenant of the hospital, the battered and wounded form of a grizzled old man, now showing faint signs of consciousness. The doctors are at work again, and the lady of the General bends over the old body, watching hopefully the returning sparks of life, and feeling that her long vigil is nearly at end, and that she can soon dismiss her faithful guard, for whom she feels more solicitude than for herself. More stimulants are administered.

She bends down and raises the old head, bolstering it up with a roll of blankets, and sees the closed eyes open and shut again. Thank God, in his goodness, it is only a question of time! When the eyes reopen, she is chafing one cold hand between her warm palms. The patient makes a weak effort to move, and utters a snarling groan, delightful to the ear of the doctor. Then the doctor redoubles his efforts, vigorously rubbing and slapping the patient's sound leg. With persistent effort he has drawn off the sodden boot, to find—a leg of *cork !*

"That beats the record," cried the exhausted medical man.

"Shut up !" growled the patient. And then, his eyes resting on the lady, and his crooked fingers closing around her hand, "Jack's Emily, by G—!"

And then she recognizes Colonel Robert ——, C.S.A., dearest friend of the General, and what should she do at last but break down in a flood of tears !

"Call in the guard, Emily," said the old man ; "the fight's over. I want t' see a United—States—soldier once more."

Then the old veterans come trooping around the dying Colonel, C.S.A., their dumb eyes full of sympathy.

Clinging with his left hand to the hand of Emily, widow of his dearest old friend, he stretches his right to the nearest old soldier, grasping with all his poor power.

"Comrades," said the Colonel, " you— were born on—the right—side. For God's sake—boys—old boys—stand shoulder—to— shoulder—for the—old flag. God bless you !

Emily— Jack's— Emily—I'm— going— lay—
me—by—Jack.''

And so the two officers of the old army sleep
shoulder to shoulder at last, in the village by
the sea, watched over by the dearest friend of
both, and yearly strewn with roses and flowers
of the magnolia and orange.

The Adventures of Certain Prisoners

THE ADVENTURES OF CERTAIN PRISONERS

IT was past noon of the first day of the bloody contest in the Wilderness. The guns of the Fifth Corps, led by Battery D of the 1st New York Artillery, were halted along the Orange turnpike, by which we had made the fruitless campaign to Mine Run. The continuous roar of musketry in front and to the left indicated that the infantry was desperately engaged, while the great guns filling every wooded road leading up to the battle-field were silent. Our drivers were lounging about the horses, while the cannoneers lay on the green grass by the roadside or walked by the pieces. Down the line came an order for the centre section, under my command, to advance and pass the right section, which lay in front of us. General Warren, surrounded by his staff, sat on a gray horse at the right of the road where the woods bordered an open field dipping between two wooded ridges. The position we were leaving was admirable, while

267

the one to which we were ordered, on the opposite side of the narrow field, was wholly impracticable. The captain had received his orders in person from General Warren, and joined my command as we passed.

We dashed down the road at a trot, the cannoneers running beside their pieces. At the centre of the field we crossed by a wooden bridge over a deep, dry ditch, and came rapidly into position at the side of the turnpike and facing the thicket. As the cannoneers were not all up, the captain and I dismounted and lent a hand in swinging round the heavy trails. The air was full of minié-balls, some whistling by like mad hornets, and others, partly spent, humming like big nails. One of the latter struck my knee with force enough to wound to the bone without penetrating the grained-leather boot - leg. In front of us the ground rose into the timber where our infantry was engaged. It was madness to continue firing here, for my shot must first plough through our own lines before reaching the enemy. So after one discharge the captain ordered the limbers to the rear, and the section started back at a gallop. My horse was cut on the flanks, and his plunging, with my disabled knee, delayed me in mounting, and prevented my seeing why the carriages kept to the grass instead of getting upon the roadway. When I overtook the guns they had come to a forced halt at the dry ditch, now full of skulkers, an angle of which cut the way to the bridge. Brief as the interval had been, not a man of my command was in sight. The lead horse of the gun team at my side had been shot and was reeling in the harness. Slipping to the ground, I untoggled one trace at the collar to release him, and had placed my hand on the other when I heard the demand "Surrender!" and turning found in my face two big pistols in the hands of an Alabama colonel. "Give me that sword," said he. I pressed the clasp and let it fall to the ground, where it remained. The colonel had taken me by the right arm, and as we turned toward the road I took in the whole situation at a glance. My chestnut horse and the captain's bald-faced brown were dashing frantically against the long, swaying gun teams. By the bridge stood a company of the 61st Alabama Infantry in butternut suits and slouch hats, shooting straggling and wounded Zouaves from a Pennsylvania brigade as they appeared in groups of two or three on the road in front. The colonel as he handed me over to his men ordered his troops to take what prisoners they could and to cease firing. The guns which we were forced to abandon were a bone of contention until they were secured by the enemy on the third day, at which time but one of the twenty-four team horses was living.

With a few other prisoners I was led by a short detour through the woods. In ten minutes we had turned the flank of both armies and reached the same turnpike in the rear of our enemy. A line of ambulances was moving back on the road, all filled with wounded, and when we saw a vacant seat beside a driver I was hoisted up to the place. The boy driver was in a high state of excitement. He said that two shells had come flying down this same road and showed where the trace of the near mule had been cut by a piece of shell, for which I was directly responsible.

The field hospital of General Jubal Early's corps was near Locust Grove Tavern, where the wounded Yankees were in charge of Surgeon Donnelly of the Pennsylvania Reserves. No guard was established, as no one was supposed to be in condition to run away. At the end of a week, however, my leg had greatly improved, although I was still unable to use it. In our party was another lieutenant, an aide on the staff of General James C. Rice, whose horse had been shot under him while riding at full speed with despatches. Lieutenant Hadley had returned to consciousness to find himself a prisoner in hospital, somewhat bruised, and robbed of his valuables, but not otherwise disabled. We two concluded to start for Washington by way of Kelly's Ford. I traded my penknife for a haversack of corn-bread with one of the Confederate nurses, and a wounded officer, Colonel Miller of a New York regiment, gave us a pocket compass. I provided myself with a stout pole, which I used with both hands in lieu of my left foot. At 9 P.M. we set out, passing during the night the narrow field and the dry ditch where I had left my guns. Only a pile of dead horses marked the spot.

On a grassy bank we captured a firefly and shut him in between the glass and the face of our pocket compass. With such a guide we shaped our course for the Rapidan. After travelling nearly all night we lay down exhausted upon a bluff within sound of the river and slept until sunrise. Hastening to our feet again, we hurried down to the ford. Just before reaching the river we heard shouts behind us and saw a man beckoning and running after us. Believing the man an enemy, we dashed into the shallow water, and after crossing safely hobbled away up the other side as fast as a man with one leg and a pole could travel. I afterward met this man, himself a prisoner, at Macon, Ga. He was the officer of our pickets, and would have conducted us into our lines if we had permitted him to come up with us. As it was, we found a snug hiding-place in a thicket of swamp growth, where we lay in concealment all day. After struggling on a few miles in a chilling rain my leg became so painful that it was impossible to go farther. A house was near by, and we threw ourselves on the mercy of the family. Good Mrs. Brandon had harbored the pickets of both armies again and again, and had luxuriated in real coffee and tea and priceless salt at the hands of our officers. She bore the Yankees only good-will, and after dressing my wound we sat down to breakfast with herself and her daughters.

After breakfast we were conducted to the second half-story, which was one unfinished room. There was a bed in one corner where we were to sleep. Beyond the stairs was a pile of yellow ears of corn, and from the rafters and sills hung a variety of dried herbs and medicinal roots. Here our meals were served, and the girls brought us books and read aloud to pass away the long days. I was confined to

the bed, and my companion never ventured below stairs except on one dark night, when at
my earnest entreaty he set out for Kelly's Ford,
but soon returned, unable to make his way in
the darkness. One day we heard the door
open at the foot of the stairs, a tread of
heavy boots on the steps, and the clank,
clank of something that sounded very much
like a sabre. Out of the floor rose a gray
slouch hat with the yellow cord and tassel of
a cavalry-man, and in another moment there
stood on the landing one of the most astonished troopers that ever was seen. " Coot "
Brandon was one of " Jeb " Stuart's rangers,
and came every day for corn for his horse.
Heretofore the corn had been brought down
for him, and he was as ignorant of our presence as we were of his existence. On this
day no pretext could keep him from coming
up to help himself. His mother worked
on his sympathies, and he departed prom-
ising her that he would leave us undisturbed.
But the very next morning he turned up
again, this time accompanied by another
ranger of sterner mold. A parole was exacted
from my able-bodied companion and we were
left for another twenty-four hours, when I was
considered in condition to be moved. Mrs.

Brandon gave us each a new blue overcoat from a plentiful store of Uncle Sam's clothing she had on hand, and I opened my heart and gave her my last twenty-dollar greenback—and wished I had it back again every day for the next ten months.

I was mounted on a horse, and with Lieutenant Hadley on foot we were marched under guard all day until we arrived at a field hospital established in the rear of Longstreet's corps, my companion being sent on to some prison for officers. Thence I was forwarded with a train-load of wounded to Lynchburg, on which General Hunter was then marching, and we had good reason to hope for a speedy deliverance. On more than one day we heard his guns to the north, where there was no force but a few citizens with bird-guns to oppose the entrance of his command. The slaves were employed on a line of breastworks which there was no adequate force to hold. It was our opinion that one well-disciplined regiment could have captured and held the town. It was several days before a portion of General Breckinridge's command arrived for the defence of Lynchburg.

I had clung to my clean bed in the hospital just as long as my rapidly healing wound would permit, but was soon transferred to a prison where at night the sleepers—Yankees, Confederate deserters, and negroes—were so crowded upon the floor that some lay under the feet of the guards in the doorways. The atmosphere was dreadful. I fell ill, and for three days lay with my head in the fireplace, more dead than alive.

A few days thereafter about three hundred prisoners were crowded into cattle cars bound for Andersonville. We must have been a week on this railroad journey when an Irish lieutenant of a Rochester regiment and I, who had been allowed to ride in the baggage car, were taken from the train at Macon, Ga., where about sixteen hundred Union officers were confined at the Fair Grounds. General Alexander Shaler, of Sedgwick's corps, also captured at the Wilderness, was the ranking officer, and to him was accorded a sort of interior command of the camp. Before passing through the gate we expected to see a crowd bearing some outward semblance of respectability. Instead, we were instantly surrounded by several hundred ragged, bare-footed, frowsy-headed men shouting "Fresh fish!" at the top of their voices and eagerly asking for news. With rare exceptions all were shabbily dressed. There was, however, a little knot of naval officers, who had been captured in the windings of the narrow Rappahannock by a force of cavalry, and who were the aristocrats of the camp. They were housed in a substantial fair-building in the centre of the grounds, and by some special terms of surrender must have brought their complete wardrobes along. On hot days they appeared in spotless white duck, which they were permitted to send outside to be laundered. Their mess was abundantly supplied with the fruits and vegetables of the season. The ripe red tomatoes they were daily seen to peel were the envy of the camp. I well remember that to me, at this time, a favorite occupation was to lie on my back with closed eyes and imagine the dinner I would order if I were in a first-class hotel. It was no unusual thing to see a dignified colonel washing his lower clothes in a pail, clad only in his uniform dress-coat. Ladies sometimes appeared on the guard-walk outside the top of the stockade, on which occasions the cleanest and best-dressed men turned out to see and be seen. I was quite proud to appear in a clean gray shirt, spotless white drawers, and mocassins made of blue overcoat cloth.

On the Fourth of July, after the regular morning count, we repaired to the big central building and held an informal celebration. One officer had brought into captivity, concealed on his person, a little silk national flag, which was carried up into the cross-beams of the building, and the sight of it created the wildest enthusiasm. We cheered the flag and applauded the speeches until a detachment of the guard succeeded in putting a stop to our proceedings. They tried to capture the flag, but in this they were not successful. We were informed that cannon were planted commanding the camp, and would be opened on us if we renewed our demonstrations. '

Soon after this episode the fall of Atlanta and the subsequent movements of General Sherman led to the breaking up of the camp at Macon, and to the transfer of half of us to a camp at Charleston and half to Savannah. Late in September, by another transfer, we found ourselves together again at Columbia. We had no form of shelter, and there was no stockade around the camp, only a guard and a dead-line. During two hours of each morning an extra line of guards was stationed around an adjoining piece of pine woods, into which we were allowed to go and cut wood and timber to construct for ourselves huts for the approaching winter. Our ration at this time consisted of raw corn-meal and sorghum molasses, without salt or any provision of utensils for cooking. The camp took its name from our principal article of diet, and was by common consent known as " Camp Sorghum." A stream of clear water was accessible during the day by an extension of the guards, but at night the lines were so contracted as to leave the path leading to the water outside the guard. Lieutenant S. H. M. Byers, who had already written the well-known lyric " Sherman's March to the Sea," was sharing my tent, which consisted of a ragged blanket. We had been in the new camp but little more than a week when we determined to make an attempt at escape. Preparatory to starting we concealed two tin cups and two blankets in the pine woods to which we had access during the chopping hours, and here was to be our rendezvous in case we were separated in getting out. Covering my shoulders with an old gray blanket and providing myself with a stick from the woodpile about the size of a gun, I tried to smuggle myself into the relief guard when the line was contracted at six o'clock. Unfortunately an unexpected halt was called, and the soldier in front turned and discovered me. I was now more than ever determined on getting away. After a hurried conference with Lieutenant Byers, at

which I promised to wait at our rendezvous in
the woods until I heard the posting of the ten
o'clock relief, I proceeded alone up the side of
the camp to a point where a group of low cedars
grew close to the dead-line. Concealing myself in their dark shadow, I could observe at my
leisure the movements of the sentinels. A full
moon was just rising above the horizon to my
left, and in the soft, misty light the guards were
plainly visible for a long distance either way.
An open field from which the small growth had
been recently cut away lay beyond, and between
the camp and the guard-line ran a broad road
of soft sand—noiseless to cross, but so white in
the moonlight that a leaf blown across it by the
wind could scarcely escape a vigilant eye. The
guards were bundled in their overcoats, and I
soon observed that the two who met opposite
to my place of concealment turned and walked
their short beats without looking back. Waiting until they separated again, and regardless of
the fact that I might with equal likelihood be
seen by a dozen sentinels in either direction, I
ran quickly across the soft sand road several
yards into the open field, and threw myself down
upon the uneven ground. First I dragged my
body on my elbows for a few yards, then I crept
on my knees, and so gradually gained in dis-

tance until I could rise to a standing position and get safely to the shelter of the trees. With some difficulty I found the cups and blankets we had concealed, and lay down to await the arrival of my companion. Soon I heard several shots which I understood too well; and, as I afterward learned, two officers were shot dead for attempting the feat I had accomplished, and perhaps in emulation of my success. A third young officer, whom I knew, was also killed in camp by one of the shots fired at the others.

At ten o'clock I set out alone and made my way across the fields to the banks of the Saluda, where a covered bridge crossed to Columbia. Hiding when it was light, wandering through fields and swamps by night, and venturing at last to seek food of negroes, I proceeded for thirteen days toward the sea.

In general I had followed the Columbia turn-pike; at a quaint little chapel on the shore of Goose Creek, but a few miles out of Charleston, I turned to the north and bent my course for the coast above the city. About this time I learned that I should find no boats along the shore between Charleston and the mouth of the Santee, everything able to float having been destroyed to prevent the escape of the negroes and the desertion of the soldiers. I was ferried over the Broad River by a crusty old darky who came paddling across in response to my cries of "O-v-e-r," and who seemed so put out because I had no fare for him that I gave him my case-knife. The next evening I had the only taste of meat of this thirteen days' journey, which I got from an old negro whom I found alone in his cabin eating possum and rice.

I had never seen the open sea-coast beaten by the surf, and after being satisfied that I had no hope of escape in that direction it was in part my curiosity that led me on, and partly a vague idea that I would get Confederate transportation back to Columbia and take a fresh start westward bound. The tide was out, and in a little cove I found an abundance of oysters bedded in the mud, some of which I cracked with stones and ate. After satisfying my hunger, and finding the sea rather unexpectedly tame inside the line of islands which marked the eastern horizon, I bent my steps toward a fire, where I found a detachment of Confederate coast-guards, to whom I offered myself as a guest as coolly as if my whole toilsome journey had been prosecuted to that end.

In the morning I was marched a few miles to Mount Pleasant, near Fort Moultrie, and taken thence in a sail-boat across the harbor to Charleston. At night I found myself again in the city jail, where with a large party of officers I had spent most of the month of August. My cellmate was Lieutenant H. G. Dorr of the 4th Massachusetts Cavalry, with whom I journeyed by rail back to Columbia, arriving at "Camp Sorghum" about the 1st of November.

I rejoined the mess of Lieutenant Byers and introduced to the others Lieutenant Dorr, whose cool assurance was a prize that procured us all the blessings possible. He could borrow frying-pans from the guards, money from his brother Masons at headquarters, and I believe if we had asked him to secure us a gun he would have charmed it out of the hand of a sentinel on duty.

Lieutenant Edward E. Sill, of General Daniel Butterfield's staff, whom I had met at Macon, during my absence had come to "Sorghum" from a fruitless trip to Macon for exchange, and I had promised to join him in an escape when he could secure a pair of shoes. On the 29th of November our mess had cut down a big pine-tree and had rolled into camp a short section of the trunk, which a Tennessee officer was to split into shingles to complete our hut, a pretty good cabin with earthen fireplace. While we were resting from our exertion, Sill appeared with his

friend Lieutenant A. T. Lamson of the 104th
New York Infantry, and reminded me of my
promise. The prisoners always respected their
parole on wood-chopping expeditions, and went
out and came in at the main entrance. The
guards were a particularly verdant body of back
country militia, and the confusion of the parole
system enabled us to practice ruses. In our
present difficulty we resorted to a new expedient
and forged a parole. The next day all three of
us were quietly walking down the guard-line on
the outside. At the creek, where all the camp
came for water, we found Dorr and Byers and
West, and calling to one of them in the presence
of the guard asked for blankets to bring in spruce
boughs for beds. When the blankets came
they contained certain haversacks, cups, and little indispensable articles for the road. Falling
back into the woods, we secured a safe hiding-
place until after dark. Just beyond the village
of Lexington we successfully evaded the first
picket, being warned of its presence by the
smoldering embers in the road. A few nights
after this, having exposed ourselves and antici-
pating pursuit, we pushed on until we came to
a stream crossing the road. Up this we waded
for some distance and secured a hiding-place on
a neighboring hill. In the morning we looked

out upon mounted men and dogs, at the very
point where we had entered the stream, searching for our lost trail. We spent two days, during
a severe storm of rain and sleet, in a farm barn
where the slaves were so drunk on applejack
that they had forgotten us and left us with nothing to eat but raw turnips. One night, in our
search for provisions, we met a party of negroes
burning charcoal who took us to their camp
and sent out for a supply of food. While waiting a venerable "uncle" proposed to hold a
prayer-meeting. So, under the tall trees and
by the light of the smoldering coal-pits, the old
man prayed long and fervently to the "bressed
Lord and Massa Lincoln," and hearty amens
echoed through the woods. Besides a few small
potatoes, one dried goat ham was all our zeal-
ous friends could procure. The next day, having made our camp in the secure depths of a
dry swamp, we lighted the only fire we allowed
ourselves between Columbia and the mountains.
The ham, which was almost as light as cork,
was riddled with worm holes, and as hard as a
petrified sponge.

We avoided the towns, and after an endless
variety of adventures approached the mountains, cold, hungry, ragged, and footsore. On
the night of December 13th we were grouped

about a guide-post, at a fork in the road, earnestly contending as to which way we should proceed. Lieutenant Sill was for the right, I was for the left, and no amount of persuasion could induce Lieutenant Lamson to decide the controversy. I yielded, and we turned to the right. After walking a mile in a state of general uncertainty we came to a low white farmhouse standing very near to the road. It was now close upon midnight and the windows were all dark, but from a house of logs, partly behind the other, gleamed a bright light. Judging this to be servants' quarters, two of us remained back while Lieutenant Sill made a cautious approach. In due time a negro appeared, advancing stealthily, and, beckoning to my companion and me, conducted us in the shadow of a hedge to a side window, through which we clambered into the cabin. We were made very comfortable in the glow of a bright wood fire. Sweet potatoes were already roasting in the ashes, and a tin pot of barley coffee was steaming on the coals. Rain and sleet had begun to fall, and it was decided that after having been warmed and refreshed we should be concealed in the barn until the following night. Accordingly we were conducted thither and put to bed upon a pile of corn-shucks high up under the roof. Secure as this retreat seemed, it was deemed advisable in the morning to burrow several feet down in the mow, so that the children, if by any chance they should climb so high, might romp unsuspecting over our heads. We could still look out through the cracks in the siding and get sufficient light whereby to study a map of the Southern States, which had been brought us with our breakfast. A luxurious repast was in preparation, to be eaten at the quarters before starting, but a frolic being in progress, and a certain negro present of questionable fidelity, the banquet was transferred to the barn. The great barn doors were set open, and the cloth was spread on the floor by the light of the moon. Certainly we had partaken of no such substantial fare within the Confederacy. The central dish was a pork pie, flanked by savory little patties of sausage. There were sweet potatoes, fleecy biscuits, a jug of sorghum, and a pitcher of sweet milk. Most delicious of all was a variety of cornbread, having tiny bits of fresh pork baked in it, like plums in a pudding.

Filling our haversacks with the fragments, we took grateful leave of our sable benefactors and resumed our journey, retracing our steps to the point of disagreement of the evening before.

Long experience in night marching had taught us extreme caution. We had advanced along the new road but a short way when we were startled by the barking of a house dog. Apprehending that something was moving in front of us, we instantly withdrew into the woods. We had scarcely concealed ourselves when two cavalrymen passed along, driving before them a prisoner. Aware that it was high time to betake ourselves to the cross-roads and describe a wide circle around the military station at Pickensville, we first sought information. A ray of light was visible from a hut in the woods, and believing from its humble appearance that it sheltered friends, my companions lay down in concealment while I advanced to reconnoitre. I gained the side of the house, and looking through a crack in the boards saw, to my horror, a soldier lying on his back before the fire and playing with a dog. I stole back with redoubled care. Thoroughly alarmed by the dangers we had already encountered, we decided to abandon the roads. Near midnight of December 16th we passed through a wooden gate on a level road leading into the forest. Believing that the lateness of the hour would secure us from further dangers, we resolved to press on with all speed, when two figures with lighted torches came suddenly into view. Knowing that we were yet unseen, we turned into the woods and concealed ourselves behind separate trees at no great distance from the path. Soon the advancing lights revealed two hunters, mere lads, but having at their heels a pack of mongrel dogs, with which they had probably been pursuing the coon or the possum. The boys would have passed unaware of our presence, but the dogs, scurrying along with their noses in the leaves, soon struck our trail and were instantly yelping about us. We had possessed ourselves of the name of the commanding officer of the neighboring post at Pendleton, and advanced boldly, representing ourselves to be his soldiers. "Then where did you get them blue pantaloons?" they demanded, exchanging glances, which showed they were not ignorant of our true character. We coolly faced them down and resumed our march leisurely, while the boys still lingered undecided. When out of sight we abandoned the road and fled at the top of our speed. We had covered a long distance through forest and field before we heard in our wake the faint yelping of the pack. Plunging into the first stream, we dashed for some distance along its bed. Emerging on the opposite bank, we sped on through marshy fields, skirting high hills and bounding down through dry watercourses, over shelving stones and accumulated barriers of driftwood ; now panting up a steep ascent, and now resting for a moment to rub our shoes with the resinous needles of the pine ; always within hearing of the dogs, whose fitful cries varied in volume in accordance with the broken conformation of the intervening country. Knowing that in speed and endurance we were no match for our four-footed pursuers, we trusted to our precautions for throwing them off the scent, mindful that they were but an ill-bred kennel and the more easily to be disposed of. Physically we were capable of prolonged exertion. Fainter and less frequent came the cry of the dogs, until, ceasing altogether, we were assured of our escape.

At Oconee, on Sunday, December 18th, we met a negro well acquainted with the roads and passes into North Carolina, who furnished us information by which we travelled for two nights, recognizing on the second objects which by his direction we avoided, like the house of Black Bill McKinney, and going directly to that of friendly old Tom Handcock. The first of these two nights we struggled up the foot-hills and outlying spurs of the mountains, through an uninhabited waste of rolling barrens, along an old stage road, long deserted, and in places impassable to a saddle mule. Lying down before morning, high up on the side of the mountain, we fell asleep, to be awakened by thunder and lightning and to find torrents of hail and sleet beating upon our blankets. Chilled to the bone, we ventured to build a small fire in a secluded place. After dark, and before abandoning our camp, we gathered quantities of wood, stacking it upon the fire, which when we left it was a wild tower of flame lighting up the whole mountain side in the direction we had come, and seeming, in some sort, to atone for a long succession of shivering days in fireless bivouac. We followed the same stage road through the scattering settlement of Casher's Valley in Jackson County, North Carolina. A little farther on, two houses, of hewn logs, with verandas and green blinds, just fitted the description we had received of the home of old Tom Handcock. Knocking boldly at the door of the farther one, we were soon in the presence of the loyal mountaineer. He and his wife had been sleeping on a bed spread upon the floor before the fire. Drawing this to one side, they heaped the chimney with green wood and were soon listening with genuine delight to the story of our adventures.

After breakfast next day, Tom, with his rifle, led us by a back road to the house of " 'Squire Larkin C. Hooper," a leading loyalist, whom we met on the way, and together we proceeded to his house. Ragged and forlorn, we were eagerly welcomed at his home by Hooper's invalid wife and daughters. For several days we enjoyed a hospitality given as freely to utter strangers as if we had been relatives of the family.

Here we learned of a party about to start through the mountains for East Tennessee, guided by Emanuel Headen, who lived on the crest of the Blue Ridge. Our friend Tom was to be one of the party, and other refugees were coming over the Georgia border, where Headen, better known in the settlement as " Man Heady," was mustering his party. It now being near Christmas, and the 'squire's family in daily expectation of a relative, who was a captain in the Confederate army, it was deemed prudent for us to go on to Headen's under the guidance of Tom. Setting out at sunset on the 23d of December, it was late in the evening when we arrived at our destination, having walked nine miles up the mountain trails over

a light carpeting of snow. Pausing in front of
a diminutive cabin, through the chinks of
whose stone fireplace and stick chimney the
whole interior seemed to be red hot like a fur-
nace, our guide demanded, " Is Man Heady
to hum?" Receiving a sharp negative in
reply, he continued, " Well, can Tom get to
stay all night?" At this the door flew open
and a skinny woman appeared, her home-spun
frock pendent with tow-headed urchins.

"In course you can," she cried, leading the
way into the cabin. Never have I seen so
unique a character as this voluble, hatchet-
faced, tireless woman. Her skin was like yellow
parchment, and I doubt if she knew by experience what it was to be sick or weary. She
had built the stake-and-cap fences that divided
the fields, and she boasted of the acres she had
ploughed. The cabin was very small. Two
bedsteads, with a narrow alleyway between,
occupied half the interior. One was heaped
with rubbish and in the other slept the whole
family, consisting of father, mother, a daughter
of sixteen, and two little boys. When I add
that the room contained a massive timber loom,
a table, a spinning wheel, and a variety of rude
seats, it will be understood that we were
crowded uncomfortably close to the fire.

Shrinking back as far as possible from the blaze, we listened in amused wonder to the tongue of this seemingly untamed virago, who, nevertheless, proved to be the kindest-hearted of women. She cursed, in her high-pitched tones, for a pack of fools, the men who had brought on the war. Roderic Norton, who lived down the mountain, she expressed a profane desire to " stomp through the turnpike," because at some time he had stolen one of her hogs, marked, as to the ear, with " two smooth craps an' a slit in the left." Once only she had journeyed into the low country, where she had seen those twin marvels, steam cars and brick chimneys. On this occasion she had driven a heifer to market, making a journey of forty miles, walking beside her horse and wagon, which she took along to bring back the corn-meal received in payment for the animal. Charged by her husband to bring back the heifer bell, and being denied that musical instrument by the purchaser, it immediately assumed more importance to her mind than horse, wagon, and corn-meal. Baffled at first, she proceeded to the pasture in the gray of the morning, cornered the cow and cut off the bell, and, in her own picturesque language, " walked through the streets of Walhalla cussin'." Rising at midnight she would fall to spinning with all her energy. To us, waked from sleep on the floor by the humming of the wheel, she seemed by the light of the low fire like a witch in a sunbonnet, darting forward and back.

We remained there several days, sometimes at the cabin and sometimes at a cavern in the rocks such as abound throughout the mountains, and which are called by the natives "rock houses." Many of the men at that time were "outliers"—that is, they camped in the mountain fastnesses, receiving their food from some member of the family. Some of these men, as now, had their copper stills in the rock houses, while others, more wary of the recruiting sergeant, wandered from point to point, their only furniture a rifle and a bedquilt. On December 29th, we were joined at the cavern by Lieutenant Knapp and Captain Smith, Federal officers, who had also made their way from Columbia, and by three refugees from Georgia, whom I remember as Old Man Tigue and the two Vincent boys. During the night our party was to start across the mountains for Tennessee. Tom Handcock was momentarily expected to join us. Our guide was busy with preparations for the journey. The night coming on icy cold, and a cutting wind driving the smoke of

the fire into our granite house, we abandoned it
at nine o'clock and descended to the cabin.
Headen and his wife had gone to the mill for a
supply of corn-meal. Although it was time for
their return, we were in no wise alarmed by
their absence, and formed a jovial circle about
the roaring chimney. About midnight came a
rap on the door. Thinking it was Tom Handcock and some of his companions, I threw it
open with an eager " Come in, boys ! " The
boys began to come in, stamping the snow from
their boots and rattling their muskets on the
floor, until the house was full, and yet others
were on guard without and crowding the porch.
" Man Heady " and his wife were already
prisoners at the mill, and the house had been
picketed for some hours awaiting the arrival of
the other refugees, who had discovered the plot
just in time to keep out of the toils. Marshalled
in some semblance of military array, we were
marched down the mountain, over the frozen
ground, to the house of old Roderic Norton.
The Yankee officers were sent to an upper
room, while the refugees were guarded below,
under the immediate eyes of the soldiery.
Making the best of our misfortune, our original
trio bounced promptly into a warm bed, which
had been recently deserted by some mem-

bers of the family, and secured a good night's rest.

Lieutenant Knapp, who had imprudently indulged in frozen chestnuts on the mountain side, was attacked with violent cramps, and kept the household below stairs in commotion all night humanely endeavoring to assuage his agony. In the morning, although quite recovered, he cunningly feigned a continuance of his pains, and was left behind in the keeping of two guards, who having no suspicion of his deep designs left their guns in the house and went out to the spring to wash. Knapp, instantly on the alert, possessed himself of the muskets, and breaking the lock of one, by a powerful effort he bent the barrel of the other, and dashed out through the garden. His keepers, returning from the spring, shouted and rushed indoors only to find their disabled pieces. They joined our party later in the day, rendering a chapfallen account of their detached service.

We had but a moderate march to make to the headquarters of the battalion, where we were to spend the night. Our guards we found kindly disposed toward us, but bitterly upbraiding the refugees, whom they saluted by the ancient name of Tories. Lieutenant Cogdill, in command of the expedition, privately informed us that his sympathies were entirely ours, but as a matter of duty he should guard us jealously while under his military charge. If we could effect our escape thereafter we had only to come to his mountain home and he would conceal us until such time as he could despatch us with safety over the borders. These mountain soldiers were mostly of two classes, both opposed to the war, but doing home-guard duty in lieu of sterner service in the field. Numbers were of the outlier class, who, wearied of continual hiding in the laurel brakes, had embraced this service as a compromise. Many were deserters, some of whom had coolly set at defiance the terms of their furloughs, while others had abandoned the camps in Virginia, and, versed in mountain craft, had made their way along the Blue Ridge and put in a heroic appearance in their native valleys.

That night we arrived at a farm-house near the river, where we found Major Parker, commanding the battalion, with a small detachment, billeted upon the family. The farmer was a gray-haired old loyalist, whom I shall always remember, leaning on his staff in the middle of the kitchen, barred out from his place in the chimney-corner by the noisy circle

of his unbidden guests. Major Parker was a
brisk little man, clad in brindle jeans of an
ancient cut, resplendent with brass buttons.
Two small piercing eyes, deep-set beside a
hawk's-beak nose, twinkled from under the rim
of his brown straw hat, whose crown was de-
fiantly surmounted by a cock's feather. But
he was exceedingly jolly withal and welcomed
the Yankees with pompous good - humor, despatching a sergeant for a jug of apple-jack,
which was doubtless as inexpensive to the major as his other hospitality. Having been a
prisoner at Chicago, he prided himself on his
knowledge of dungeon etiquette and the military courtesies due to our rank.

We were awakened in the morning by high-
pitched voices in the room below. Lieutenant
Sill and I had passed the night in neighboring
caverns of the same miraculous feather-bed.
We recognized the voice of the major, inform-
ing some culprit that he had just ten minutes
to live, and that if he wished to send any dying
message to his wife or children then and there
was his last opportunity; and then followed
the tramping of the guards as they retired from
his presence with their victim. Hastily dressing, we hurried down to find what was the
matter. We were welcomed with a cheery

good-morning from the major, who seemed to be in the sunniest of spirits. No sign of commotion was visible. "Step out to the branch, gentlemen; your parole of honor is sufficient; you'll find towels—been a prisoner myself." And he restrained by a sign the sentinel who would have accompanied us. At the branch, in the yard, we found the other refugees trembling for their fate, and learned that Headen had gone to the orchard in the charge of a file of soldiers with a rope. While we were discussing the situation and endeavoring to calm the apprehensions of the Georgians the executioners returned from the orchard, our guide marching in advance and looking none the worse for the rough handling he had undergone. The brave fellow had confided his last message and been thrice drawn up toward the branch of an apple tree, and as many times lowered for the information it was supposed he would give. Nothing was learned, and it is probable he had no secrets to disclose or conceal.

Lieutenant Cogdill, with two soldiers, was detailed to conduct us to Quallatown, a Cherokee station at the foot of the Great Smoky Mountains. Two horses were allotted to the guard, and we set out in military order, the refugees two and two in advance, Headen and

Old Man Tigue lashed together by the wrists, and the rear brought up by the troopers on horseback. It was the last day of the year, and although a winter morning, the rare mountain air was as soft as spring. We struck the banks of the Tuckasegee directly opposite to a feathery waterfall, which, leaping over a crag of the opposite cliff, was dissipated in a glittering sheet of spray before reaching the tops of the trees below. As the morning advanced we fell into a more negligent order of marching. The beautiful river, a wide, swift current, flowing smoothly between thickly wooded banks, swept by on our left, and on the right wild, uninhabited mountains closed in the road. The two Vincents were strolling along far in advance. Some distance behind them were Headen and Tigue; the remainder of us following in a general group, Sill mounted beside one of the guards. Advancing in this order, a cry from the front broke on the stillness of the woods, and we beheld Old Man Tigue gesticulating wildly in the centre of the road and screaming, "He's gone! He's gone! Catch him!" Sure enough the old man was alone, the fragment of the parted strap dangling from his outstretched wrist. The guard, who was mounted, dashed off in pursuit, followed by the lieutenant on foot, but both soon returned, giving over the hopeless chase. Thoroughly frightened by the events of the morning, Headen [1] had watched his opportunity to make good his escape, and as we afterward learned, joined by Knapp and Tom Handcock, he conducted a party safely to Tennessee.

At Webster, the court town of Jackson County, we were quartered for the night in the jail, but accompanied Lieutenant Cogdill to a venison breakfast at the parsonage with Mrs. Harris and her daughter, who had called on us the evening before. Snow had fallen during the night, and when we continued our march it was with the half-frozen slush crushing in and out, at every step, through our broken shoes. Before the close of this dreary New Year's day we came upon the scene of one of those wild tragedies which are still of too frequent occurrence in those remote regions, isolated from the strong arm of the law. Our road led down and around the mountain side, which on our right was a barren, rocky waste, sloping gradually up

[1] A short time ago the writer received the following letter: "Casher's Valley, May 28, 1890. Old Manuel Headen and wife are living, but separated. Julia Ann is living with her mother. The old lady is blind. Old man Norton (Roderic), to whose house you were taken as prisoner, has been dead for years. Old Tom Handcock is dead.—W. R. Hooper."

from the inner curve of the arc we were describing. From this direction arose a low wailing sound, and a little farther on we came in view of a dismal group of men, women, and mules. In the centre of the gathering lay the lifeless remains of a father and his two sons; seated upon the ground, swaying and weeping over their dead, were the mother and wives of the young men. A burial party, armed with spades and picks, waited by their mules, while at a respectful distance from the mourners stood a circle of neighbors and passers-by, some gazing in silent sympathy, and others not hesitating to express a quiet approval of the shocking tragedy. Between two families, the Hoopers and the Watsons, a bitter feud had long existed, and from time to time men of each clan had fallen by the rifles of the other. The Hoopers were loyal Union men, and if the Watsons yielded any loyalty it was to the State of North Carolina. On one occasion shortly before the final tragedy, when one of the young Hoopers was sitting quietly in his door, a light puff of smoke rose from the bushes and a rifle ball ploughed through his leg. The Hoopers resolved to begin the new year by wiping out their enemies, root and branch. Before light they had surrounded the log cabin of the Watsons and secured all the male inmates, except one who, wounded, escaped through a window. The latter afterward executed a singular revenge, by killing and skinning the dog of his enemies and elevating the carcass on a pole in front of their house.

After a brief stay at Quallatown we set out for Asheville, leaving behind our old and friendly guard. Besides the soldiers who now had us in charge, a Cherokee Indian was allotted to each prisoner, with instructions to keep his man constantly in view. To travel with an armed Indian, sullen and silent, trotting at your heels like a dog, with very explicit instructions to blow out your brains at the first attempt to escape, is neither cheerful nor ornamental, and we were a sorry-looking party plodding silently along the road. Detachments of prisoners were frequently passed over this route, and regular stopping-places were established for the nights. It was growing dusk when we arrived at the first cantonment, which was the wing of a great barren farm-house owned by Colonel Bryson. The place was already occupied by a party of refugees, and we were directed to a barn in the field beyond. We had brought with us uncooked rations, and while two of the soldiers went into the house for cooking utensils, the rest of the party, including the Indians, were leaning in a line upon the dooryard fence ; Sill and Lamson were at the end of the line, where the fence cornered with a hedge. Presently the two soldiers reappeared, one of them with an iron pot in which to cook our meat, and the other swinging in his hand a burning brand. In the wake of these guides we followed down to the barn, and had already started a fire when word came from the house that for fear of rain we had best return to the corn-barn. It was not until we were again in the road that I noticed the absence of Sill and Lamson. I hastened to Smith and confided the good news. The fugitives were missed almost simultaneously by the guards, who first beat up the vicinity of the barn, and then, after securing the remainder of us in a corn - crib, sent out the Indians in pursuit. Faithful dogs, as these Cherokees had shown themselves during the day, they proved but poor hunters when the game was in the bush, and soon returned, giving over the chase. Half an hour later they were all back in camp, baking their hoecake in genuine aboriginal fashion, flattened on the surface of a board and inclined to the heat of the fire.[1]

[1] Sill and Lamson reached Loudon, Tenn., in February. A few days after their escape from the Indian guard they

That I was eager to follow goes without saying, but our keepers had learned our slippery character. All the way to Asheville, day and night, we were watched with sleepless vigilance. There we gave our parole, Smith and I, and secured thereby comfortable quarters in the courthouse, with freedom to stroll about the town. Old Man Tigue and the Vincents were committed to the county jail. We were there a week, part of my spare time being employed in helping a Confederate company officer make out a correct pay-roll.

When our diminished ranks had been recruited by four more officers from Columbia, who had been captured near the frozen summit of the Great Smoky Mountains, we were started on a journey of sixty miles to Greenville in South Carolina. The night before our arrival we were quartered at a large farm-house. The

arrived at the house of " Shooting John Brown," who confided them to the care of the young Hoopers and a party of their outlying companions. From a rocky cliff overlooking the valley of the Tuckasegee they could look down on the river roads dotted with the sheriff's posse in pursuit of the Hoopers. So near were they that they could distinguish a relative of the Watsons leading the sheriff's party. One of the Hooper boys, with characteristic recklessness and to the consternation of the others, stood boldly out on a great rock in plain sight of his pursuers (if they had chanced to look up), half resolved to try his rifle at the last of the Watsons.

prisoners, together with the privates of the guard, were allotted a comfortable room, which contained, however, but a single bed. The officer in charge had retired to enjoy the hospitality of the family. A flock of enormous white pullets were roosting in the yard. Procuring an iron kettle from the servants, who looked with grinning approval upon all forms of chicken stealing, we sallied forth to the capture. Twisting the precious necks of half a dozen, we left them to die in the grass while we pierced the side of a sweet-potato mound. Loaded with our booty we retreated to the house undiscovered, and spent the night in cooking in one pot instead of sleeping in one bed. The fowls were skinned instead of plucked, and, vandals that we were, dressed on the backs of the picture frames, taken down from the walls.

At Greenville we were lodged in the county jail to await the reconstruction of railway bridges, when we were to be transported to Columbia. The jail was a stone structure, two stories in height, with halls through the centre on both floors and square rooms on each side. The lock was turned on our little party of six in one of these upper rooms, having two grated windows looking down on the walk. Through the door which opened on the hall a square hole

was cut as high as one's face and large enough
to admit the passage of a plate. Aside from
the rigor of our confinement we were treated
with marked kindness. We had scarcely walked
about our dungeon before the jailer's daughters
were at the door with their autograph albums.
In a few days we were playing draughts and
reading Bulwer, while the girls, without, were
preparing our food and knitting for us warm
new stockings. Notwithstanding all these at-
tentions we were ungratefully discontented. At
the end of the first week we were joined by
seven enlisted men, Ohio boys, who like ourselves had been found at large in the mountains.
From one of these new arrivals we procured a
case-knife and a gun screw-driver. Down on
the hearth before the fire the screw-driver was
placed on the thick edge of the knife, and be-
labored with a beef-bone until a few inches of
its back were converted into a rude saw. The
grate in the window was formed of cast-iron
bars, passing perpendicularly through wrought-
iron plates, bedded in the stone jambs. If one
of these perpendicular bars, an inch and a half
square, could be cut through, the plates might
be easily bent so as to permit the egress of a
man. With this end in view we cautiously began operations. Outside of the bars a piece of

carpet had been stretched to keep out the raw wind, and behind this we worked with safety. An hour's toil produced but a few feathery filings on the horizontal plate, but many hands make light work, and steadily the cut grew deeper. We recalled the adventures of Claude Duval, Dick Turpin, and Sixteen-string Jack, and sawed away. During the available hours of three days and throughout one entire night the blade of steel was worrying, rasping, eating the iron bar. At last the grosser yielded to the temper and persistence of the finer metal. It was Saturday night when the toilsome cut was completed, and preparations were already under way for a speedy departure. The jail had always been regarded as too secure to require a military guard, although soldiers were quartered in the town ; besides, the night was so cold that a crust had formed on the snow, and both citizens and soldiers, unused to such extreme weather, would be likely to remain indoors. For greater secrecy of movement, we divided into small parties, aiming to traverse different roads. I was to go with my former companion, Captain Smith. Lots were cast to determine the order of our going. First exit was allotted to four of the Ohio soldiers. Made fast to the grating outside were a bit of rope and strip of blankets, along which to descend. Our room was immediately over that of the jailer and his sleeping family, and beneath our opening was a window, which each man must pass in his descent. At eleven o'clock the exodus began. The first man was passed through the bars amid a suppressed buzz of whispered cautions. His boots were handed after him in a haversack. The rest of us, pressing our faces to the frosty grating, listened breathlessly for the success of the movement we could no longer see. Suddenly there was a crash, and in the midst of mutterings of anger we snatched in the rag ladder and restored the piece of carpeting to its place outside the bars. Our pioneer had hurt his hand against the rough stones, and, floundering in mid-air, had dashed his leg through sash and glass of the window below. We could see nothing of his further movements, but soon discovered the jailer standing in the door, looking up and down the street, seemingly in the dark as to where the crash came from. At last, wearied and worried and disappointed, we lay down in our blankets upon the hard floor.

At daylight we were awakened by the voice of Miss Emma at the hole in the door, "Who got out last night?" "Welty." "Well, you was fools you didn't all go ; pap wouldn't 'a' stopped you. If you'll keep the break concealed until night we'll let you all out.'' The secret of the extreme kindness of our keepers was explained. The jailer, a loyalist, retained his position as a civil detail, thus protecting himself and sons from conscription. Welty had been taken in the night before, his bruises had been anointed, and he had been provisioned for the journey.

We spent the day repairing our clothing and preparing for the road. My long-heeled cowhides, '' wife's shoes,'' for which I had exchanged a uniform waistcoat with a cottonwooled old darky on the banks of the Saluda, were about parting soles from uppers, and I kept the twain together by winding my feet with stout cords. At supper an extra ration was given us. As soon as it was dark the old jailer appeared among us and gave us a minute description of the different roads leading west into the mountains, warning us of certain dangers. At eleven o'clock Miss Emma came with the great keys, and we followed her, in single file, down the stairs and out into the back yard of the jail. From the broken gratings in front, the bit of rope and strips of blanket were left dangling in the wind.

We made short work of leave-taking, Captain
Smith and I separating immediately from the
rest, and pushing hurriedly out of the sleeping
town, by back streets, into the bitter cold of the
country roads. We stopped once to warm at
the pits of some negro charcoal burners, and
before day dawned had travelled sixteen miles.
We found a sheltered nook on the side of the
mountain open to the sun, where we made a
bed of dry leaves and remained for the day.
At night we set out again, due west by the
stars, but before we had gone far my companion,
who claimed to know something of the country,
insisted upon going to the left, and within a
mile turned into another left-hand road. I
protested, claiming that this course was leading
us back. While we were yet contending we
came to a bridgeless creek whose dark waters
barred our progress, and at the same moment,
as if induced by the thought of the fording, the
captain was seized with rheumatic pains in his
knees, so that he walked with difficulty. We
had just passed a house where lights were still
showing, and to this we decided to return, hoping at least to find shelter for Smith. Leaving
him at the gate, I went to a side porch and
knocked at the door, which was opened by a
woman who proved to be friendly to our cause,

her husband being in the rebel army much
against his will. We were soon seated to the
right and left of her fireplace. Blazing pine-
knots brilliantly lighted the room, and a number of beds lined the walls. A trundle-bed before the fire was occupied by a very old woman
who was feebly moaning with rheumatism.
Our hostess shouted into the old lady's ear,
"Granny, them's Yankees." "Be they!"
said she, peering at us with her poor old eyes.
"Be ye sellin' tablecloths?" When it was
explained that we were just from the war, she
demanded, in an absent way, to know if we were
Britishers. We slept in one of the comfortable
beds, and as a measure of prudence passed the
day in the woods, leaving at nightfall with
well-filled haversacks. Captain Smith was again
the victim of his rheumatism, and directing me
to his friends at Cæsar's Head, where I was to
wait for him until Monday (it then being Tuesday), he returned to the house, little thinking
that we were separating forever.

I travelled very rapidly all night, hoping to
make the whole distance, but day was breaking
when I reached the head waters of the Saluda.
Following up the stream I found a dam on which
I crossed, and although the sun was rising and
the voices of children mingled with the lowing

of cattle in the frosty air, I ran across the
fields and gained a secure hiding-place on the
side of the mountain. It was a long, solitary
day, and glad was I when it grew sufficiently
dark to turn the little settlement and get into
the main road up the mountain. It was six
zigzag miles to the top, the road turning on log
abutments, well anchored with stones, and not
a habitation on the way until I should reach
Bishop's house, on the crest of the divide.
Half way up I paused before a big summer hotel, looming up in the woods like the ghost of a
deserted factory, its broken windows and rot-
ting gateways redoubling the solitude of the
bleak mountain side. Shortly before reaching
Bishop's, " wife's shoes " became quite unman-
ageable. One had climbed up my leg half way
to the knee, and I knocked at the door with
the wreck of the other in my hand. My visit
had been preceded but a day by a squad of partisan raiders, who had carried away the bedding
and driven off the cattle of my new friends, and
for this reason the most generous hospitality
could offer no better couch than the hard floor.
Stretched thereon in close proximity to the dying fire, the cold air coming up through the
wide cracks between the hewn planks seemed to
be cutting me in sections as with icy saws, so

that I was forced to establish myself lengthwise of a broad puncheon at the side of the room and under the table.

In this family " the gray mare was the better horse," and poor Bishop, an inoffensive man, and a cripple withal, was wedded to a regular Xantippe. It was evident that unpleasant thoughts were dominant in the woman's mind as she proceeded sullenly and vigorously with preparations for breakfast. The bitter bread of charity was being prepared with a vengeance for the unwelcome guest. Premonitions of the coming storm flashed now and then in lightning cuffs on the ears of the children, or crashed venomously among the pottery in the fireplace. At last the repast was spread, the table still standing against the wall, as is the custom among mountain housewives. The good-natured husband now advanced cheerfully to lend a hand in removing it into the middle of the room. It was when one of the table legs overturned the swill-pail that the long pent-up storm burst in a torrent of invective. The prospect of spending several days here was a very gloomy outlook, and the relief was great when it was proposed to pay a visit to Neighbor Case, whose house was in the nearest valley, and with whose sons Captain Smith had lain

in concealment for some weeks on a former visit to the mountains. I was curious to see his
sons, who were famous outliers. From safe
cover they delighted to pick off a recruiting officer or a tax-in-kind collector, or tumble out
of their saddles the last drivers of a wagon train.
These lively young men had been in unusual
demand of late and their hiding-place was not
known even to the faithful, so I was condemned
to the society of an outlier of a less picturesque
variety. Pink Bishop was a blacksmith, and
just the man to forge me a set of shoes from the
leather Neighbor Case had already provided.
The little still-shed, concealed from the road
only by a low hill, was considered an unsafe
harbor, on account of a fresh fall of snow with
its sensibility to tell-tale impressions. So we
set up our shoe factory in a deserted cabin, well
back on the mountain and just astride of that
imaginary line which divides the Carolinas.
From the fireplace we dug away the cornstalks,
heaping the displaced bundles against broken
windows and windy cracks, and otherwise secured our retreat against frost and enemies.
Then ensued three days of primitive shoemak-
ing. As may be inferred, the shoes made no
pretension to style. I sewed the short seams at
the sides and split the pegs from a section of

seasoned maple. Rudely constructed as these shoes were they bore their wearer triumphantly into the promised land.

I restrained my eagerness to be going until Monday night, the time agreed upon, when, my disabled companion not putting in an appearance, I set out for my old friend's in Casher's Valley. I got safely over a long wooden bridge within half a mile of a garrisoned town. I left the road, and turned, as I believed, away from the town, but I was absolutely lost in the darkness of a snow-storm, and forced to seek counsel as well as shelter. In this plight I pressed on toward a light, glimmering faintly through the blinding snow. It led me into the shelter of the porch to a small brown house, cut deeply beneath the low eaves and protected at the sides by flanking bedrooms. My knock was answered by a girlish voice, and from the ensuing parley, through the closed door, I learned that she was the daughter of a Baptist exhorter, and that she was alone in the house, her brother away at the village, and her father, having preached the day before at some distance, was not expected home until the next morning. Reassured by my civil-toned inquiries about the road, she unfastened the door and came out to the porch, where she proceeded to instruct me how to go on, which was just the thing I least desired to do. By this time I had discovered the political complexion of the family, and, making myself known, was instantly invited in, with the assurance that her father would be gravely displeased if she permitted me to go on before he returned. I had interrupted my little benefactress in the act of writing a letter, on a sheet of foolscap, which lay on an old-fashioned stand in one corner of the room beside the ink-bottle and the candlestick. In the diagonal corner stood a tall bookcase, the crowded volumes nestling lovingly behind the glass doors—the only collection of the sort that I saw at any time in the mountains. A feather-bed was spread upon the floor, the head raised by means of a turned-down chair, and here I was reposing comfortably when the brother arrived. It was late in the forenoon when the minister reached home, his rickety wagon creaking through the snow, and drawn at a snail's pace by a long-furred, knock-kneed horse. The tall but not very clerical figure was wrapped in a shawl and swathed round the throat with many turns of a woollen tippet. The daughter ran out with eagerness to greet her father and tell of the wonderful arrival. I was received with genuine delight. It was the enthusiasm of a patriot, eager to find a sympathetic ear for his long-repressed views.[1]

When night came and no entreaties could prevail to detain me over another day, the minister conducted me some distance in person, passing me on with ample directions to another exhorter, who was located for that night at the house of a miller who kept a ferocious dog. I came first to the pond and then to the mill, and got into the house without encountering the dog. Aware of the necessity of arriving before bedtime, I had made such speed as to find the miller's family still lingering about the fireplace with preacher number two seated in the lay circle. That night I slept with the parson, who sat up in bed in the morning, and after disencumbering himself of a striped extinguisher nightcap electrified the

[1] The Rev. James H. Duckworth, now postmaster of Brevard, Transylvania County, North Carolina, and in 1868 member of the State Constitutional Convention, in his letter of June 24, 1890, says: " I have not forgotten those things of which you speak. I can almost see you (even in imagination) standing at the fire when I drove up to the gate and went into the house and asked you, ' Have I ever seen you before?' Just then I observed your uniform. ' Oh, yes,' said I ; ' I know who it is now.' . . . This daughter of whom you speak married about a year after, and is living in Morgantown, North Carolina, about one hundred miles from here. Hattie (for that is her name) is a pious, religious woman."

other sleepers by announcing that this was the
first time he had ever slept with a Yankee.
After breakfast the parson, armed with staff
and scrip, signified his purpose to walk with
me during the day, as it was no longer dangerous to move by daylight. We must have been
travelling the regular Baptist road, for we
lodged that night at the house of another lay
brother. The minister continued with me a
few miles in the morning, intending to put me
in the company of a man who was going
toward Casher's Valley on a hunting expedition. When we reached his house, however,
the hunter had gone ; so, after parting with
my guide, I set forward through the woods,
following the tracks of the hunter's horse. The
shoe-prints were sometimes plainly impressed
in the snow, and again for long distances over
dry leaves and bare ground, but an occasional
trace could be found. It was past noon when
I arrived at the house where the hunters were
assembled. Quite a number of men were
gathered in and about the porch, just returned
from the chase. Blinded by the snow over
which I had been walking in the glare of the
sun, I blundered up the steps, inquiring without much tact for the rider who had preceded
me, and was no little alarmed at receiving a

rude and gruff reception. I continued in suspense for some time until my man found an opportunity to inform me that there were suspicious persons present, thus accounting for his unexpected manner. The explanation was made at a combination meal, serving for both dinner and supper, and consisting exclusively of beans. I set out at twilight to make a walk of thirteen miles to the house of our old friend Esquire Hooper. Eager for the cordial welcome which I knew awaited me, and nerved by the frosty air, I sped over the level wood-road, much of the way running instead of walking. Three times I came upon bends of the same broad rivulet. Taking off my shoes and stockings and rolling up my trousers above my knees, I tried the first passage. Flakes of broken ice were eddying against the banks, and before gaining the middle of the stream my feet and ankles ached with the cold, the sharp pain increasing at every step until I threw my blanket on the opposite bank and springing upon it wrapped my feet in its dry folds. Rising a little knoll soon after making the third ford, I came suddenly upon the familiar stopping-place of my former journey. It was scarcely more than nine o'clock, and the little hardships of the journey from Cæsar's

Head seemed but a cheap outlay for the joy of the meeting with friends so interested in the varied fortunes of myself and my late companions. Together we rejoiced at the escape of Sill and Lamson, and made merry over the vicissitudes of my checkered career. Here I first learned of the safe arrival in Tennessee of Knapp, Man Heady, and Old Tom Handcock.

After a day's rest I climbed the mountains to the Headen cabin, now presided over by the heroine of the heifer bell in the absence of her fugitive husband. Saddling her horse, she took me the next evening to join a lad who was about starting for Shooting Creek. Young Green was awaiting my arrival, and after a brief delay we were off on a journey of something like sixty miles; the journey, however, was pushed to a successful termination by the help of information gleaned by the way. It was at the close of the last night's march, which had been long and uneventful, except that we had surmounted no fewer than three snow - capped ridges, that my blacksmith's shoes, soaked to a pulp by the wet snow, gave out altogether. On the top of the last ridge I found myself panting in the yellow light of the rising sun, the sad wrecks of my two shoes dangling from my hands, a wilderness of beauty spread out before me, and a sparkling field of frosty forms beneath my tingling feet. Stretching far into the west toward the open country of East Tennessee was the limitless wilderness of mountains drawn like mighty furrows across the toilsome way, the pale blue of the uttermost ridges fading into an imperceptible union with the sky. A log house was in sight down in the valley, a perpendicular column of smoke rising from its single chimney. Toward this we picked our way, I in my stocking feet, and my boy guide confidently predicting that we should find the required cobbler. Of course we found him in a country where every family makes its own shoes as much as its own bread, and he was ready to serve the traveller without pay. Notwithstanding our night's work, we tarried no longer than for the necessary repairs, and just before sunset we looked down upon the scattering settlement of Shooting Creek. Standing on the bleak brow of " Chunky Gall " Mountain, my guide recognized the first familiar object on the trip, which was the roof of his uncle's house. At Shooting Creek I was the guest of the Widow Kitchen, whose house was the principal one in the settlement and whose estate boasted two slaves. The husband had fallen by an anonymous bullet while salting his cattle on the mountain in an early year of the war.

On the day following my arrival I was conducted over a ridge to another creek, where I met two professional guides, Quince Edmonston and Mack Hooper. As I came upon the pair parting a thicket of laurel, with their long rifles at a shoulder, I instantly recognized the coat of the latter as the snuff-colored sack in which I had last seen Lieutenant Lamson. It had been given to the man at Chattanooga, where these same guides had conducted my former companions in safety a month before. Quince Edmonston, the elder, had led numerous parties of Yankee officers over the Wacheesa trail for a consideration of a hundred dollars, pledged to be paid by each officer at Chattanooga or Nashville.

Two other officers were concealed near by, and a number of refugees, awaiting a convoy, and an arrangement was rapidly made with the guides. The swollen condition of the Valley River made it necessary to remain for several days at Shooting Creek before setting out. Mack and I were staying at the house of Mrs. Kitchen. It was on the afternoon of a memorable Friday, the rain still falling in torrents without, that I sat before the fire poring over a small Sunday-school book ; the only printed book in the house, if not in the settlement. Mack Hooper was sitting by the door. Attracted by a rustling sound in his direction, I looked up just in time to see his heels disappearing under the nearest bed. Leaping to my feet with an instinctive impulse to do likewise, I was confronted in the doorway by a stalwart Confederate officer fully uniformed and armed. Behind him was his quartermaster sergeant. This was a Government party collecting the tax-in-kind, which at that time throughout the Confederacy was the tenth part of all crops and other farm productions. It was an ugly surprise. Seeing no escape, I ventured a remark on the weather ; only a stare in reply. A plan of escape flashed through my mind like an inspiration. I seated myself quietly, and for an instant bent my eyes upon the printed pages. The two soldiers had advanced to the corner of the chimney nearest the door, inquiring for the head of the family and keeping their eyes riveted on my hostile uniform. At this juncture I was seized with a severe fit of coughing. With one hand upon my chest, I walked slowly past the men, and laid my carefully opened book face down upon a chest. With another step or two I was in the porch, and bounding into the kitchen I sprang out through a window already opened by the women for my exit. Away I sped bareheaded through the pelting rain, now crashing through thick underbrush, and now to my waist in swollen streams, plunging on and on, only mindful to select a course that would baffle horsemen in pursuit. After some miles of running I took cover behind a stack, within view of the road which Mack must take in retreating to the other settlement ; and sure enough here he was, coming down the road with my cap and haversack, which was already loaded for the western journey. Mack had remained undiscovered under the bed, an interested listener to the conversation that ensued. The officer had been assured that I was a friendly scout ; but convinced of the contrary by my flight, he had departed swearing he would capture that Yankee before morning if he had to search the whole settlement. So alarmed were we for our safety that we crossed that night into a third valley and slept in the loft of a horse-barn.

On Sunday our expedition assembled on a hillside overlooking Shooting Creek, where our friends in the secret of the movement came up to bid us adieu. With guides we were a party of thirteen or fourteen, but only three of us officers who were to pay for our safe conduct. Each man carried his supply of bread and meat and bedding. Some were wrapped in faded bedquilts and some in tattered army blankets ; nearly all wore ragged clothes, broken shoes, and had unkempt beards. We arrived upon a mountain side overlooking the settlement of Peach Tree, and were awaiting the friendly shades of night under which to descend to the house of the man who was to put us across Valley River. Premature darkness was accompanied with torrents of rain, through which we followed our now uncertain guides. At last the light of the cabin we were seeking gleamed humidly through the trees. Most of the family fled into the outhouses at our approach, some of them not reappearing until we were disposed for sleep in a half-circle before the fire. The last arrival were two tall women in homespun dresses and calico sun-bonnets. They slid timidly in at the door, with averted faces, and then with a rush and a bounce covered themselves out of sight in a bed, where they had probably been sleeping in the same clothing when we approached the house. Here we learned that a cavalcade of four hundred Texan Rangers had advanced into Tennessee by the roads on the day before. Our guides. familiar with the movements of these dreaded troopers, calculated that with the day's delay enforced by the state of the river a blow would have been struck and the marauders would be in full retreat before we should arrive on the ground. We passed that day concealed in a stable, and as soon as it was sufficiently dark we proceeded in a body to the bank of the river attended by a man and a horse. The stream was narrow, but the current was full and swift. The horse breasted the flood with difficulty, but he bore us all across one at a time, seated behind the farmer.

We had now left behind us the last settlement, and before us lay only wild and uninhabited mountains. The trail we travelled was an Indian path extending for nearly seventy miles through an uninhabited wilderness. Instead of crossing the ridges it follows the trend of the range, winding for the most part along the crests of the divides. The occasional traveller having once mounted to its level pursues his solitary way with little climbing.

Early in the morning of the fourth day our little party was assembled upon the last mountain overlooking the open country of East Tennessee. Some of us had been wandering in the mountains for the whole winter. We were returning to a half-forgotten world of farms and fences, roads and railways. Below us stretched the Tellico River away toward the line of towns marking the course of the Nashville and Chattanooga Railroad. One of the guides who had ventured down to the nearest house returned with information that the four hundred Texan Rangers had burned the depot at Philadelphia Station the day before, but were now thought to be out of the country. We could see the distant smoke arising from the ruins. Where the river flowed out of the mountains were extensive iron-works, the property of a loyal citizen, and in front of his house we halted for consultation. He regretted that we had shown ourselves so soon, as the rear guard of the marauders had passed the night within sight of where we now stood. Our nearest pickets were at Loudon, thirty miles distant on the railway, and for this station we were advised to make all speed.

For half a mile the road ran along the bank of the river and then turned around a wooded bluff to the right. Opposite to this bluff and accessible by a shallow ford was another hill, where it was feared that some of the Rangers were still lingering about their camp. As we came to the turn in the road our company was

walking rapidly in Indian file, guide Edmonston and I at the front. Coming around the
bluff from the opposite direction was a coun-
tryman mounted on a powerful gray mare.
His overcoat was army blue, but he wore a
bristling fur cap, and his rifle was slung on his
back. At sight of us he turned in his saddle
to shout to some one behind, and bringing his
gun to bear came tearing and swearing down
the road, spattering the gravel under the big
hoofs of the gray. Close at his heels rode two
officers in Confederate gray uniforms, and a
motley crowd of riders closed up the road behind. In an instant the guide and I were surrounded, the whole cavalcade levelling their
guns at the thicket and calling on our companions to halt, who could be plainly heard
crashing through the bushes. The dress of
but few of our captors could be seen, nearly
all being covered with rubber talmas, but their
mounts, including mules as well as horses, were
equipped with every variety of bridle and saddle to be imagined. I knew at a glance that
this was no body of our cavalry. If we were
in the hands of the Rangers the fate of the
guides and refugees would be the hardest. I
thought they might spare the lives of the officers. "Who are you? What are you doing

here?" demanded the commander, riding up
to us and scrutinizing our rags. I hesitated a
moment, and then, throwing off the blanket I
wore over my shoulders, simply said, "You
can see what I am." My rags were the rags
of a uniform, and spoke for themselves.

Our captors proved to be a company of the
2d Ohio Heavy Artillery, in pursuit of the marauders into whose clutches we thought we had
fallen. The farmer on the gray mare was the
guide of the expedition, and the two men uniformed as rebel officers were Union scouts.
The irregular equipment of the animals, which
had excited my suspicion most, as well as the
animals themselves, had been hastily impressed
from the country about the village of London,
where the 2d Ohio was stationed. On the following evening, which was the 4th of March,
the day of the second inauguration of President Lincoln, we walked into London and
gladly surrendered ourselves to the outposts of
the Ohio Heavy Artillery.